Praise for the Kenni Lowry Mystery Series

FIXIN' TO DIE (#1)

"Packed with clever plot twists, entertaining characters, and plenty of red herrings! *Fixin' To Die* is a rollicking, delightful, down-home mystery."

— Ann Charles,
USA Today Bestselling Author of the Deadwood Mystery Series

"Southern and side-splitting funny! *Fixin' To Die* has captivating characters, nosy neighbors, and is served up with a ghost and a side of murder."

— Duffy Brown,
Author of the Consignment Shop Mysteries

"A Southern-fried mystery with a twist that'll leave you positively breathless."

— Susan M. Boyer,
USA Today Bestselling Author of *Lowcountry Book Club*

"This first book in a new series promises to be fun for both cozy mystery buffs and ghost aficionados."

— *For The Love of Books*

D0870685

FIXIN' TO
DIE

The Kenni Lowry Mystery Series
by Tonya Kappes

FIXIN' TO DIE (#1)

FIXIN' TO
DIE
A KENNI LOWRY MYSTERY

TONYA KAPPES

HENERY PRESS

FIXIN' TO DIE
A Kenni Lowry Mystery
Part of the Henery Press Mystery Collection

First Edition | June 2016

Henery Press, LLC
www.henerypress.com

This is a work of fiction. Any references to historical events, real people, or real locales are used fictitiously. Other names, characters, places, and incidents are the product of the author's imagination, and any resemblance to actual events or locales or persons, living or dead, is entirely coincidental.

Trade Paperback ISBN-13: 978-1-63511-037-1
Digital epub ISBN-13: 978-1-63511-038-8
Kindle ISBN-13: 978-1-63511-039-5
Hardcover Paperback ISBN-13: 978-1-63511-040-1

Printed in the United States of America

*With love to my small hometown of Nicholasville.
Late at night when I sit with my quiet mind, I can recall all the wonderful memories, small town love, and charm that helped me write the fictional town of Cottonwood.*

Chapter One

"Calling all units. Calling all units." Betty Murphy's voice felt like a stiletto in my ear as it came over the police walkie-talkie.

The clock read seven in the morning. Betty couldn't have been at the sheriff's office long enough to already be calling all units.

Not a good sign for a Monday morning. I had yet to enjoy my cup of coffee.

"Damn," I groaned, putting the coffee cup in the beanbag coffee holder that laid over the hump on the floorboard. It was too early for anyone in Cottonwood, Kentucky to be out and about, much less needing assistance from the sheriff's department. Well, unless it was about the multiple coyote sightings that had been reported throughout the county, which weren't unusual for this time of the year. In that case, I had my twelve gauge nestled on the backseat, ready to scare them away.

Duke lunged his front paws from the passenger side to the floorboard, licking up what little coffee had spilled. There was no way he was getting all of his ninety-pound body squeezed down on the floorboard.

"Kenni, you there?" Betty asked again before I could un-Velcro the walkie-talkie from my shoulder. "Calling all units."

I wasn't sure why she'd be calling for all units when the only unit was me, and Betty was well aware of that fact. Holding the steering wheel steady with one hand, I reached up and grabbed the police radio.

"Betty, I'm here." I twisted the windshield wipers on to get what was hopefully the last of the lingering rain we'd had over the past few days. "What do you have for me?"

"Oh God, Kenni." She sounded out of breath, rushing over my nickname, short for Kendrick. "I mean, Sheriff Lowry. I barely got in the door and put my pocketbook down before the phone started ringing." She didn't skip a beat. "Ronald Walton is dead and you better get over there before the rest of the town hears about it and beats you there."

I jerked forward when I brought the old Wagoneer to an abrupt stop. I scooted up on the edge of my seat and looked out the windshield and over the hood to make sure the engine wasn't lying on the pavement.

"What?" Shock came over me. I stared out the window. Betty had to be mistaken.

Doctor Walton had birthed over ninety-five percent of the population in Cottonwood, including me. He was old, but not casket-shopping old. And his death would be a blow to the community.

"D-E-A-D!" She spit out each letter for me as if I didn't know how to spell. She sucked in a deep breath. "Where are you?" Betty asked through her sobs.

"I'm out on Bone Road going toward the festival grounds to make sure they haven't flooded." I swung the Jeep around and headed back to town. The unseasonable amount of rain had calmed to a slow drizzle. "I'm on my way." My voice cracked with weariness.

I had just seen Doc Walton a couple of weeks ago for my annual physical and he'd looked healthy to me. "Gosh, I hope he didn't have a heart attack."

"What do you mean, heart attack?" Betty talked so fast, her false teeth clicked. "He is knife-sticking-out-of-his-neck dead. Far from a heart attack." Her voice choked. "I'm talking murder."

"M...M..." I couldn't bring the word to form on my lips. I tried again. "Murdered?" I whispered in disbelief. "Betty, you need to call the state reserves. We are going to need some help."

There hadn't been a murder—or really any crime, for that matter—on my watch since I had been elected sheriff two years ago for a four-year term. The state reserve officers were available to small towns to help out with crime scenes like this. Especially when the town only required one sheriff and one deputy.

I pushed the gas pedal down, picking up a lot more speed. The scenery passing by was particularly dreary, as it had been just over two years ago when I had found Poppa dead of a heart attack while I was home for a visit.

"Toots Buford found him this morning when she got to work and immediately called 911," Betty said, referring to Doc's receptionist.

"Call her back and tell her I'm on my way," I said, dread in my gut. "I also need you to call Wyatt Granger. He's probably home, so wake him up and tell him to get over to Doc's because it looks like I'm going to need some help."

"Got it." Betty clicked off and I put the walkie-talkie on the seat next to me.

Air. I needed air. I cranked the handle to roll down the window.

"Stop." I pushed Duke, who would do anything to get his nose prints on my driver's side window, back over to his side of the Jeep. Not a good day to have brought him to work with me.

Stay calm.

I jerked my head around suddenly. I thought I'd heard a voice. I looked over at Duke. My eyes narrowed. The goofy dog was hanging out the window with his tongue flopping around in the wind, slobber flinging out of his mouth, splattering on the passenger window behind him.

I shook off the notion that Duke said something or I'd heard someone. I grabbed the old beacon police light, licked the suction cup, and slapped it on the roof of the Jeep, grazing the side with my finger to flip on the light and siren.

It seemed a little far-fetched that Doc Walton would be murdered. Who on earth would ever want to kill him?

The crime rate had gone down since I was elected...way down, to like none. I'd have liked to say it was because I was a known badass, but truth be told there just wasn't any crime. And my one and only deputy had recently retired and was currently on a much-needed beach vacation with his wife, or I would've called him in to help instead of Wyatt Granger, the county jailer.

The Wagoneer rattled down Poplar Holler Road, picking up speed on the downhill.

It wouldn't take me long to get to Doc's house, where he had moved his practice after I had to take away his driver's license. Cottonwood wasn't all that big. I could get from one side of town to the other in less than ten minutes.

The rain all but stopped to a slow spit just before I got to Doc's house. The old Jeep moved along Doc's dirt driveway, kicking up mud behind me.

Wyatt Granger stood in the middle of Doc Walton's yard already waiting for me. Wyatt's old Chevy Nova and Toots Buford's pink 1965 VW Bug were the only two cars there. For now.

I pulled down the visor and took a quick look in the mirror. I had planned on taking Duke home and getting a quick shower after I checked out the fairgrounds. My honey blond hair was pulled back into a loose ponytail and my day-old mascara was smudged under my eyes, creating the smoky eye look so many models seemed to want. Quickly I licked my finger and did a swipe to get off as much as I could to make myself a little more presentable.

My door swung open to Wyatt Granger standing on the other side. His wiry brows stuck up all over the place above his hooded eyes. His gray hair was cut high and tight. "You still using that old siren?"

"Still works." I shrugged, trying not to stare at his stray eyebrows. I grabbed the walkie-talkie and strapped it on my shoulder. "You got here awfully fast."

"I was just down the road when Betty called my cell. I'm glad you had her call." His hand held the driver's side door open and I grabbed my police bag from the passenger floorboard.

"What do you think we have here?" I asked.

"I'm not sure." He shook his head, his lips turned down.

"You stay," I warned Duke, and left the windows all the way down for him, even though it wasn't hot and muggy yet. I shut the door and headed toward the house with Wyatt on my heels.

"Looks like someone wanted Doc dead and didn't stick around to let us know who they are." Wyatt's head tilted to the side, shoulders shrugged. "I went ahead and made sure the premises was secured and told everyone that was here to stay put until you said it was okay for them to leave."

I listened intently to what Wyatt had to say, stopping when I saw Sterling Stinnett on Doc's porch.

"Good morning, Sterling," I said.

He stood with his hands dug deep in the front pocket of his jeans.

"Mornin', Sheriff." Sterling spoke in a low voice reserved for dreaded things. A long-time Cottonwood resident, he stood over six feet tall and his black hair was freshly slicked back. He wore his usual outfit—a two-button Henley shirt, a pair of blue jeans, and an old pair of snakeskin boots that had seen better days. "It's nice to see ya, but I sure wish it wasn't under these circumstances."

I nodded to him before I gestured for Wyatt to follow me into Doc Walton's house. I pushed open the door.

"Are you sure about this, Sheriff?" Wyatt asked, spacing his words evenly.

Before I took my first step through the door, I looked back at him. The tone in his voice infuriated me, not to mention his question.

"I mean, it's not fittin' for a girl to see a dead body." Wyatt stood firm with his hands crossed over his chest. He cleared his throat. "Besides, your daddy might kill me for letting you." He let out a long breath. He took off his John Deere cap out of southern respect. "Especially the dead body of your baby doctor. The man that helped bring you into this world."

"Then maybe the good folks of Cottonwood should've thought

about my dear old daddy when they elected me to office two years ago." I cocked my brow, giving him a "watch it" stare, daring him to say something else. I tapped the badge on the front of my brown button-up sheriff's shirt. "I assure you my father will be fine." I gripped the door handle, taking out my frustrations over Wyatt's words by giving it a good squeeze. "If you'll excuse me, I have a job to do, with or without you," I said over my shoulder, and walked into Doc Walton's house.

Wyatt followed.

I scanned the room. Toots Buford was sitting behind an old wooden desk. Her eyes were swollen and bloodshot, and her blotchy red face matched the color of her #R42 L'Oréal dye she probably bought from Dixon's Foodtown.

"I just got off the phone with Betty and we just can't believe it." She shook her head and held a ripped-up piece of toilet paper up to her face. The shredded roll sat on top of the desk.

"I bet you did." I groaned inwardly, knowing gossip around here spread like wildfire, thanks to Toots and Betty. "Where is he?" I asked, glancing around the home's family room Doc had turned into a receptionist area for his office.

Without looking up, Toots let out a sob and pointed behind her. With a few sniffs, she whispered, "First door on the right," before she planted her face back in the piece of toilet paper in her hand.

"Did you see anyone else here?" I asked. Wyatt said that he had secured the premises when he got there, but what about before? Had Toots seen anyone when she had gotten there?

"Not that I've seen." Her eyes widened at the prospect of the killer still lurking in the house somewhere.

"Please stay right here and don't touch anything." I walked around the desk and carefully stepped over the scattered files strewn on the floor.

"Take your shoes off and place them over there." Toots pointed between sobs.

"What?" I asked.

"Doc Walton doesn't let anyone wear shoes beyond this point. He says shoes carry sickness and disease on their bottoms." She sniffed, twirling around in her chair and sticking her piggies in the air and wiggling them.

"I don't believe there will be any more patients here, but for good measure." I sat my bag on top of the files on her desk and unzipped it, taking out two pairs of surgical booties and two pairs of gloves along with a couple evidence markers. I gave a set of gloves and booties to Wyatt. "Here."

I placed a couple of the evidence markers next to the papers all over the floor. In the police academy I learned that no one could ever be too cautious when it came to a crime scene.

Straight down the hall, I could see the kitchen and the back door to the house. There were two doors on each side of the hallway. I put on the gloves.

With one last look at Wyatt, I slowly turned the knob and pushed the door open, not fully prepared for what I saw.

Chapter Two

Someone had wanted to make sure Doc was dead.

"Oh, Sheriff." Wyatt let out an audible groan and slouched against the wall. He and Doc Walton were friends and I was sure it affected him on more of a personal level.

The darkness of the situation pressed down on us. My heart sank.

Doc Walton lay face down in a pool of blood. His cane was clear across the other side of the room. The blood surrounding him was a deep crimson and looked to have settled, causing me to believe he'd been there for a few hours.

The walls and floor were splattered with blood. The ticking of the second hand on the clock hanging on the wall was the only sound in the room. A veil of death curled around us as we both stood silent, sending a private prayer Doc's way.

It was still so early. I certainly wouldn't have thought Doc was open for patients at seven a.m., though he was dressed and had on his white lab coat and blue latex gloves.

I walked around his body, noticing little beads of mercury all over the floor from a broken thermometer. Small shards of glass glistened on the tile floor quite a bit away from Doc's body.

There appeared to be stab wounds on his neck, his back, and his arms. I got a good look at the ones on his neck. Whoever did this was making sure Doc Walton wasn't going to see any more patients. Ever.

I glanced around the room to see if there was a murder weapon or something that would've created the stab wounds, but nothing was visible. I crouched down and looked underneath the patient exam tables, chairs, and cabinets. There was nothing.

"Looks like somebody did him in good." Wyatt stood a little ways back from me.

"I've got it taken care of here." My hand gripped my bag. "Why don't you go on back into the office and stay with Toots? Make sure she doesn't wander around the crime scene."

Wyatt let out a heavy sigh. He wasn't used to taking orders from me. He'd been jailer as far back as I could remember.

I squatted down and took a look at the mercury beads all over the floor and was careful not to step on any.

Take an evidence sample.

"What did you say?" I looked over my shoulder at Wyatt.

"I didn't say anything." His brows drew together.

"We need to collect a few of these as evidence," I said under my breath, wondering if I had actually heard my own thoughts. There was no other explanation.

There was a protocol I had learned in the police academy when it came to a murder case, and since this was my first one, I wanted to make sure I covered all the bases.

I took my pen out of my pocket and pushed one of the mercury balls, watching it explode into tinier silver balls. I took out another evidence marker and placed it on the floor.

I put more markers next to Doc's cane, a couple more on blood splatters, and one more near the broken thermometer.

"Who's our guy?" A man's voice came from the direction of the door.

"Depends on who wants to know."

I stood up and looked at the man in the light gray suit with his black hair neatly parted to the side. He had a pair of the booties covering his shoes.

He reached in the pocket of his fancy jacket and flipped out a badge. He took a couple steps into the room, not taking his eye off Doc's body.

"Finn Vincent with the Kentucky State Reserve." He walked

over and stood next to me. "They sent me here to assist in the investigation."

"That was fast." I looked up at Doc's clock. "I just told my dispatch to call you guys in."

"I was in the next county over working with a crime over there." He glanced around the room. "Murder takes precedence over break-ins, I guess," he joked.

"Sheriff Lowry." I peeled my gloves off and stuck my hand out, giving him a nice firm handshake. "I appreciate all your help. First thing you can do is ask for Doc Walton's appointment book from the receptionist. We need to gather a list of patients and see if he had any appointments this morning. Without a motive or weapon, we need to eliminate each and every patient to narrow down a suspect list."

At this point, everyone was a suspect in my book. Including Toots and Sterling.

"He saw patients here?" Finn asked.

"Long story, but he had a fender bender a while back and had to retake the road test again because of his age. He didn't pass, so his license was revoked, but he could have retried in six months. He was still a good doctor and passed the test to keep his medical license, so he just moved his office here." I kept my eyes on him, studying his reaction.

"I'll go find that appointment book." He stepped outside the door but turned back around. "Would you like me to address the crowd outside first?"

"Crowd?" I asked.

"Yeah. It seems like your entire town is out there waiting for someone to come out and talk to them." He shrugged.

I followed behind him down the hall and took a look out the window. I shouldn't have been surprised. News traveled fast in small towns, especially ours.

"I'll go do it, Sheriff."

Wyatt walked past me and nodded his head toward Finn. They gave each other the good ole boys look.

"I'll take care of it, Wyatt. You stay here and continue to look for the weapon."

The last thing I wanted was for the town to think I was passing the ball to Wyatt. There had already been talk around town that I wasn't going to run unopposed in the next election. Plus, it wasn't a secret that some folks weren't too keen on having a woman as sheriff, but I'd have to say I'd been doing a fine job so far. I was up for re-election in two years, but politicking in small towns started two years before the actual election. I wasn't ready to give up my job, so I'd better make sure I was meeting the public's needs now.

"Are you ready?" Finn asked, his hand on the front door handle.

"As I'll ever be." My lips formed a thin line, trying to smile the best I could.

Finn was right. When he opened the door, it looked like the entire town had gathered on Doc's front lawn. They emitted a collective gasp and watched as I stepped out on the porch.

The morning was drying off; the rain had stopped. The tree branches bobbed as the wind flew across the yard, sending droplets of rain onto the crowd below.

"If I can have everyone's attention." I put my hands in the air. "I'm sure you've all heard that Doctor Ronald Walton was found deceased in his home this morning. I do not have any information on how he died, but we are treating it as a homicide at this time. There is no cause for alarm for the community. I assure you the sheriff's department has everything under control and I will keep you abreast of any and all information as I learn it. You can all go home."

Pretty pleased with my impromptu speech, I turned to go inside when I heard the raspy voice call out to me. I turned back around on instinct.

"Yoohoo!" Edna Easterly from the *Cottonwood Chronicles* scurried her way up past the crowd. A walking cliché, her brown fedora with a red polka dot ribbon around the rim sat cockeyed on her head; a big feather on the side had big globs of dried glue from a hot glue gun and a piece of paper with "reporter" written in green Sharpie marker was stuck in the front. "Sheriff Lowry!"

"Not now, Edna." My eyes lowered. "When I have more information, I'll be sure to release it to the public."

"How do you plan on handling this since Lonnie Lemar retired? Seems you are short a deputy. Your only deputy." She put her pen back on her paper ready to document my answer. "If you are here, who is going to keep the rest of Cottonwood safe?"

"This is Finn Vincent of the Kentucky Reserve Unit." I gestured toward Finn. He stood with his hands clasped in front of him. "He is here to assist until we figure out what we are going to do about filling that deputy position."

Edna's brows furrowed. "And exactly how will you be assisting?" Edna wasn't going to let the questions stop there, but I was.

"Thank you, Edna." I smiled politely. "We will let you know when we have further information."

"Is there a killer among us?" she yelled out.

I turned and headed back into the house, hoping that when I came back out the crowd would be gone, along with Edna Easterly.

"I can't believe we have a serial killer in Cottonwood." Toots began to sob all over again.

"Whoa." I put my hands out. "Who said anything about a serial killer?"

Toots let out a little sniff and shrugged.

"Let's not go packing tales where there is no tale to pack." The last thing I needed was a town full of gun-carrying people looking for a reason to shoot someone. I pointed to the stack of files. "Does your desk always look like this?"

"No." Toots shook her head. "It was like this when I got here. Sterling was outside in shock. The look on his face is forever stained on my brain." She sucked in a deep breath and slowly let it out as if she were calming herself. Her voice quivered. "I asked him what was wrong and he could only point. When I came in, I saw this and ran back to Doc. Then I called Betty. Now here you are."

I pulled the notepad and pen from the breast pocket on my shirt and flipped it open.

"Is this like one of them formal statements you see on the TV?" she asked, curling up on her toes to get a look at my notepad.

"I'm just making notes," I said to Toots, scribbling her recollection of her morning events.

I turned toward Finn. "Can you ask the gentleman in the Henley shirt on the porch to come inside?" There was no need for Sterling Stinnett to hang around. I'd get him questioned and get him on his way.

Finn walked to the door and did what I asked, coming back in with Sterling trailing behind him.

"Sterling." I waved him over. "Did you have an early appointment with Doctor Walton?"

"Nah." He shook his head. "I needed a refill on my blood pressure prescription and Doc told me to come on out when I needed it filled. I like to get here early so I can beat the heat since I have to walk."

Sterling Stinnett was sort of a drifter around Cottonwood. He had a small cement-block home with the bare necessities to live. He did odd jobs for homebuilders and some grass-cutting for the elderly.

"I knocked on the door. He usually greets me with a cup of hot coffee, but not today." He looked down at his boots and scuffed his toe on the floor. He said in a low voice, "After a few minutes, I let myself in and hollered for him."

"What time was it?" I asked, wondering how much earlier he'd gotten there before Toots.

"It was about ten minutes before Toots showed up. I was outside getting sick to my stomach after I saw Doc lying there in all that blood."

His eyes drooped, his face hollow.

"Did you touch anything while you were in here?" I asked.

"I called out his name to see if he would respond." He shook his head. "When he didn't, I walked over and bent down over him.

That's when I saw all them puncture marks in his neck and I knew he was dead."

"I'm going to need you to come down to the station and give a statement for the record and get some fingerprints taken," I told Sterling. "Maybe Wyatt can give you a ride. You can wait outside and I'll ask him."

Sterling hung his head and walked out the door. I had more questions for Toots.

"What time did you get here?" I asked Toots, trying to establish a timeline.

"It was around six forty-five." She nodded her head as though she was confirming it to herself. "Yes. Six forty-five."

"Do you always come to work this early?" I asked.

"Sometimes." She shrugged. She bit her lip and looked off in the distance. I noticed her lack of eye contact.

"What do you mean by sometimes?" I wanted a clear answer.

"Doc never gives me a set time to be here. Appointments start around nine, but sometimes people are here earlier."

"What's your morning routine?" I asked her.

"Well, I come in and grab a cup of coffee, take a look at the appointment book, and pull their files. I put the files in Doc's office, so they're there when he's ready." Her voice faded.

"What does Doc usually do while you are getting ready for the appointments?" I continued to write everything she was telling me.

"He drinks his coffee and goes through the files as I give them to him. But sometimes patients just show up like we're one of those Take Care Clinics or something." She shook her head. "And Doc never turns anyone away. Turned," she corrected her choice of words in a hushed whisper.

"Are the walk-ins added to the appointment book?" I asked, noting how this could be a crucial lead in the investigation.

"Sometimes I put them in, sometimes I don't," she said. "Depends on if they want to use insurance or some other type of payment."

"Like?" I coaxed her to continue.

"Like pie, cookies." She tilted her head and when she saw I wasn't following, she said in a whisper, "Sometimes the Sweet Adelines pay him in fresh grown veggies, bread, and sweets."

Inwardly I groaned at the word Toots seemed to love: "sometimes," but my mouth watered when she mentioned the Sweet Adelines. The group of women were not only barbershop singers who performed around Cottonwood, they also had a garden club. If you were lucky enough, and if they really liked you, your pantry was stocked full of fresh or canned vegetables all year round.

"Can you please give the appointment book to Officer Vincent?" I asked. At this point I was going to have to work with what I was given, and right now that didn't seem like much.

"What was the cleaning process around here?" If Doc was so particular about shoes, he had to be even more particular about the rest of the instruments.

"He was OCD about the place." She ripped another piece of toilet paper off the roll and dabbed the corners of her eyes. "Every time a patient left, I had to wipe down everything with Clorox."

"Every day? Every night?" I asked.

Toots nodded.

"You can go now, but I want you to stop by the station this afternoon to give a formal statement to Wyatt." With a little time between now and then, I hoped she'd remember some key information she'd forgotten in her state of shock.

My eyes slid over to Wyatt. "I'm going to see if we can get an emergency town council meeting so we can get you on as deputy until the fall election."

He nodded and tugged on the edges of his waistband. I was sure this made him happy, since I heard through the rumor mill that he was the one who wanted to run against me. After all, he was familiar with the job since the jailer's office and sheriff's office were all in one room in the back of Cowboy's Catfish Restaurant.

When a new sheriff was elected, they normally brought in their own people. Not me. I kept the deputy who was here under my Poppa when he was sheriff of Cottonwood. If Leonard was good enough for Poppa, he was certainly good enough for me. Plus, Leonard had been interim sheriff between Poppa's death and the election and he had no intentions of running. He wanted to finish out his two years and retire. I didn't blame him.

No sense in taking time to train someone new. I lived by the motto, "If it's not broke, don't try to fix it." Now that I needed a deputy, I was more than happy to appoint Wyatt to the job.

"I've got all the files." Finn held up a stack of yellow files.

I glanced around the room through hazy sadness. Wyatt, Toots, and even Finn had a deep-set pain on their faces.

"I'm afraid it's going to be a long day." I tapped the top of the files in Finn's hands. "Wyatt, cancel whatever plans you had today because I'm going to need you to head down to the station." I sucked in a deep breath. "Take Sterling with you so you can get his statement."

Everyone scattered. I stood with my hands on my hips and glared down the hallway, trying to come up with an idea of why someone would want to kill Doc Walton.

A chill swooshed down the hall and up my uniform pant leg. I took a deep breath and let out a long sigh. I wished my Poppa were here. He'd know exactly what to do next.

"Now what?" I closed my eyes and whispered, trying to channel my Poppa. "Help me, Poppa."

"You know," Finn's voice filled the space around me, an edge to it, "if you sit and listen long enough, the walls have ears. All the answers are right here. We just have to peel back the layers one at a time."

As goofy as Finn Vincent sounded, I had an eerie feeling he was right.

Chapter Three

It's one thing to learn about a murder crime scene in the police academy but a totally different experience to be thrown in the middle of one. Toots had left and Wyatt had taken Sterling in his car down to the station, leaving Finn and me alone with Doc Walton. Duke had found a spot on the corner of one of Doc's couches in the reception room—the only area we had cleared.

"Max Bogus, our county coroner and owner of our only funeral home, should be here any minute," I said to Finn and finished up writing down a few notes. "He'll do an initial assessment and then take Doc on down to the funeral home morgue."

"Any clues on who might have done this?" Finn asked.

"No idea." It was still a little shocking to me. "There hasn't been a murder here since I took office two years ago."

In the state of Kentucky, a sheriff serves a four-year term with no term limit, and I would have to say I was pretty lucky not having a murder on my watch. That lucky streak was over.

"Sheriff?" the voice of Max Bogus called from the front of the house.

"Come on in," I yelled back.

Max walked in with his brown briefcase close to his side. He wore khaki pants, a blue button-down, and thick black-rimmed glasses.

"Max, this is Finn Vincent from the Reserve Unit." I gestured between the two. "Finn, this is Max."

They gave each other a handshake and nod.

"This is a first." Max's eyes dipped, his lips pursed as he bent down over Doc's body.

"I still can't believe it. There isn't a murder weapon, which I'm assuming is a knife of some sort from all of the stab wounds," I pointed out.

"We shall see." Max held a clipboard and camera bag in his hands. "I've got to fill out the initial paperwork and you know I'll need to see any witness statements or even talk to who found him."

"Yes, of course." I nodded. "Sterling found him before Toots got here for work. You and Doc were friends; did you know he would see patients without appointments?" I asked, fearing this was going to be my biggest obstacle in the case.

"He was an old-time doctor. If someone needed to be seen, he wasn't going to turn anyone away. Not so uncommon in small towns such as Cottonwood." Max filled out the usual information on the sheet on his clipboard. Name, occupation, address of death, hair color, and clothing.

There was an outline of a dead body and he quickly made notes on the visible stab wounds. Finn and I watched as Max pulled out his camera and took pictures of Doc and all the evidence markers.

"All the puzzle pieces will fit together somehow," Max said, squatting down to get closer pictures of the mercury granules.

It was exactly what Finn had meant when he said the walls had eyes.

An hour went by before Max was ready to put Doc Walton's body on the church cart and put him in the back of the hearse. He'd taken all sorts of photos of every room in the house.

"You never know what you can find in a photo with a magnifying glass." Max's brows rose.

"Formal statements will be ready tonight. I'll get them to you when Wyatt has them typed up." A sobering feeling hit my gut as the back door of the hearse slammed shut.

"Sounds good." Max's lips pressed in a thin line. "We'll find who did this."

"I sure hope so."

I waved him off and watched him drive down the now muddy driveway.

The sun was starting to peek out. Cottonwood could use a little sunshine and much-needed relief from the rain, because the beginning of this week was turning out to be far from fun.

"I guess we can get these divided up. You take some and I'll take some." Finn walked outside with the stack of patient files.

"What do you say we grab a bite to eat?" I felt a little lightheaded and hoped it was from not eating breakfast this morning.

Finn nodded. "I could use some food."

"You can follow me to town. I know just the right place." I made sure the house was securely locked up and the police caution tape in place before I got back in the Wagoneer. "Duke! Come!"

Duke sauntered down the steps. His droopy brown eyes slid down his face, disappearing into his floppy cheeks.

I ran my hand over his light brown furry head and down his long tan ears.

"You are such a good boy." A long-needed sigh escaped my lips. Duke always made me happy. "Poppa knew what he was doing when he gave you to me."

Duke shook his flappy ears and let out a little howl as though he knew what I was saying. We got in and I put the Wagoneer in drive, watching Finn in my rearview mirror.

"Charger." I adjusted the mirror, taking a look at Finn's fancy police car. "Oh well." I rubbed the dash of my old Jeep. "We don't need a fancy car."

Duke let out another howl before he stuck his head out the window and let his ears fly in the wind.

Within a few minutes, I pulled up to the curb in front of Lulu's Boutique on the north side of town. The small boutique was really an old clapboard house turned into a cute shop owned and operated by Lulu McClain. She had local items along with knick-knacks, candles, some clothing, and other accessories for the home.

I put the Jeep in park, leaving enough room for Finn to park behind me.

Duke howled in delight when he saw the On The Run food truck. He was about to get a treat and he knew it.

On The Run, Jolee Fischer's mobile café, was parked on the side of Lulu's.

"Kenni!" Lulu trotted down the front steps of her shop looking very stylish for her age. She wore her black hair in a short, shaved Twiggy kind of way, a little longer on the top, enough to be parted on the side. Her black ruffled blouse was partially covered with a white and black speckled fur vest with leggings and knee-high black boots. Silver bangles jingled up and down her arm as she waved in the air, screaming my name. "Kenni!" There was something in her hand.

"Good morning, Ms. Lulu." I swung the Jeep door open and Duke jumped over me and out the door, bolting up to the food truck.

"Good morning." She put a little extra oomph on the "ing" in morning as her eyes rolled up and down Finn, who was next to my door before I could turn the Jeep off. "Well, it's technically early afternoon." She grinned, not taking her eyes off Finn.

"Good afternoon." Finn smiled, pulling the sunglasses off his face and hooking them in the pocket of his fancy suit coat. He ignored Lulu's lustful stares.

"Well, well. Aren't you a sight for sore eyes?" Ms. Lulu pushed between us, tucked whatever it was in her hand in her back pocket, and stuck her manicured hand out in front of her. The bracelets jingled down her arm and came to a rest on her wrist. "I'm Lulu McClain. I own Lulu's Boutique. You must be the fancy cop from out of town that everyone is talking about."

"I don't know about fancy." Finn's voice faded, losing that steely edge. "Yes, ma'am. Finn Vincent from out of town." A flash of humor crossed his face. "News travels fast."

"Faster than you know." I rolled my eyes.

"I can't help it if I called Betty Murphy to get the recipe for her chess bars. Missy Jennings is sick and I know chess bars will be just the thing to pep her up." Lulu patted her free hand over the top of Finn's hand, still shaking it like she was shaking out the water on her dishrag.

"Chess bars, huh?" Finn's mouth turned up in a big ole smile, exposing those perfect teeth.

"I'll make an extra batch." Lulu winked, still rubbing the top of his hand. "Betty told me about Doc Walton. Shame." Her brows cocked up. She heaved a deep sigh and shook her head.

"Thank you for making me some chess bars. They sound delicious." Finn's mouth was still open in a bright smile.

"Were you yelling for me?" I asked, reminding her of her frantically yelling my name when I pulled up.

Lulu cleared her throat, turning her attention to me.

"Yes, Kenni." Her face was turned toward mine, but her eyes were glued on Finn.

"Focus, Ms. Lulu."

I waved my hand in front of her.

"Oh, Kenni." She sighed, pulled the stashed item from her back pocket, and held out the thing toward me. "I know your mother would love this monogrammed scarf. It's a perfect color for her." She held it up to my face. "I mean, it looks good up to your olive skin tone and you are a mini-me of her. Plus, she does love a monogram."

I smiled a dreary smile, knowing exactly what Lulu was up to. My rocky relationship with my parents wasn't a big secret in our town—and I was sure it was a topic the circle of coffee talk shared—but Ms. Lulu was on a mission for me to reestablish the bond with my parents that came completely unglued when I decided to go to the police academy. After I graduated from the academy, I worked on the University campus police force, which I guess my mama thought was playing pretend.

When Poppa died, it was election year, so I threw my hat in and won. My mama absolutely threw a hissy fit when she found out I was running. I didn't even want to remember how she acted when

I actually won. I thought I was going to have to take her to the nearest hospital, a forty-five-minute drive east into Lexington.

"And she about died when I called her about Doc Walton—um," Lulu's eyes flew open, "I mean, when I let it slip about Doc Walton while I was telling her about Missy Jennings. Because I know she'd get a burr in her saddle if she found out some other way since she and Missy are Euchre partners."

"You let it slip, huh?" I asked in a monotone voice, knowing it was exactly why she called my mama: to stir the pot.

Lulu was definitely a good pot-stirrer.

"Why, yes." Lulu's southern drawl drew out even more, my keen judge of character telling me she was lying right there to my face. She leaned in and nudged me with her elbow, the smell of vanilla oozing from her every pore.

"Is there a serial killer among us?" she asked. "I won't tell."

"Serial killer?" Finn's smile faded. His crow's-feet deepened.

"No." I shook my head. "There is no serial killer. One killer." My face reddened. "One crime. Only one." I held my finger in the air.

"Mark my words." She stomped her fancy boot on the ground. "I told the city council one year ago not to build those condos out there by the river. I told them building those would bring all sorts of seedy people to our little town. But no." She swayed back and forth, her finger wagging in the air. She looked like she was in Beyoncé's "Single Ladies" video. Not that I was a Beyoncé fan. Not that I wasn't. "No one wanted to listen to me. And now this happens."

"Thank you for voicing your concerns. I'll be sure to put it in my notes." I had to be sure every citizen was heard. Part of the job. "I'm sure you'll see Mama before me." I tilted my head. "We have to go."

"Right. Crime to solve." Her solemn face took a turn on a dime and her sweet southern smile was right back. She turned to Finn. "Do you know who did it?"

"I'm holding you to those chess bars." He winked. She giggled.

My stomach growled.

It was my cue to leave and get in line for food. Finn could fend for himself; I left him to say goodbye to Lulu. A few minutes later he walked up next to me.

"That was wrong. All sorts of wrong," I said.

"What?" he asked in a dumbfounded voice.

"You know what. Flirting with an old lady," I growled, though I secretly found it a little endearing.

"It made her drop the questioning." He held the file up in the air, following closely behind me. "Here are the files. We can go over them at the table."

I picked up the pace. The line for On The Run was getting longer and the day was slipping away. There was a lot more I needed to get done before the sun went down.

"Nice dog." Finn laughed at Duke.

My ornery pup had made his way to the front of the line and was quickly eating up any food that accidentally fell out of the cardboard cartons Jolee used to serve it.

"Everyone knows Duke," I said.

He nodded. "Getting back to town was easier than I anticipated." Finn looked up and down Main Street. He was trying to make small talk to fill the space. "And the rain has stopped for now."

"Huh?" I asked. There were only a few streets between Doc Walton's house in the country and the town. It wasn't like Cottonwood was a big city or anything.

"When I was trying to find the crime scene, I stopped and asked someone for directions." He pulled out a piece of paper from his suit pocket. He flashed it toward me. There was some scribble on it.

"Oh no." I closed my eyes in anticipation. The way we southerners gave directions was nowhere near the fancy GPS most people used.

"I repeat, the exact directions." He held the piece of paper up to his face. He said in his best hillbilly accent, "That's way out yonder. This is what you are gonna do." He looked up at me and continued, "You are gonna drive straight down this road until you get to the outhouse on the cement blocks where there isn't a stitch of grass. Anyways, you are gonna turn right right there. Well, it's really a curve, but go slow because Grant Henry took that curve and ended up knocking that outhouse down. That's why it's on cement blocks now."

I couldn't help but laugh. Finn Vincent was getting a good dose of how the local folks gave directions. We understood yonder and down there.

"Oh, it doesn't stop there." He held the piece of paper up to his face again. "Now you are gonna keep going, keep going down a real long piece, but slow down because that girl sheriff we got will give you a ticket. Eventually there is gonna be a fork in the road, you gonna go left. Now there is a cross in the middle of the road where that fork is because someone died there, but stay left of that cross. That's the street you want because Doc Walton's house is on that street."

Finn busted out laughing, shaking his head. His eyes danced with a little twinkle and his teeth sparkled.

"You don't have a fancy GPS on your phone?" I asked, taking a step closer to the order window.

"I do, but the cell service is spotty around here." He let out a deep sigh.

"Ohio?" I asked, trying to figure out where his accent came from.

"What?" Finn's brows furrowed.

"You're from Ohio?" I asked, patting my leg for Duke to come back to me.

It only made sense that Finn was from Ohio. It wasn't too far from Cottonwood and he definitely wasn't from anywhere in Kentucky.

He shook his head. "Chicago. But I've been with the Kentucky State Police Reserve Unit for a few years now. What kind of café is this?"

"Something Jolee Fischer came up with to piss Ben Harrison off." I smiled fondly, remembering the fight the two of them had at the town council meeting. After that night, Jolee was on a mission to make Ben miserable and she was doing a pretty good job of it. "Jolee graduated from culinary school and thought she'd land a cooking job at Ben's. He handed her an apron and an ordering pad." I pointed to the yellow clapboard home behind us and then to the silver streamlined trailer. "That's when Jolee bought this camper and turned it into a food truck. Genius idea, really." I ran my hand over Duke, giving him a good scratch behind his ears, his soft spot. "She travels to local businesses and sets up shop. Like Lulu's Boutique." I pointed back to the house. "Lulu hosts a crochet class, knitting class, beading class...come to think of it, she teaches a lot of classes." I waved my hand in the air, trying to forget I had my monthly Euchre group coming up.

They would definitely bombard me with questions about the murder, plus my mama would be there. Maybe not, since Missy Jennings was ill.

"Jolee shows up with little goodies for them to buy and take into class. She just kinda shows up everywhere. With the right permits, of course." I made sure he knew I was doing everything right so he couldn't go back to the state police and say I wasn't doing my job. Not that I would care, it just wasn't a hassle I needed.

"How does this work here?" Finn looked at his fancy gold watch I was sure didn't come from the local Walmart.

"You order from Jolee's food truck and take it into Lulu's craft room to eat at one of the tables. The two of them have some sort of commission percentage worked out. This way Jolee doesn't have the overhead a restaurant would." It all made perfect sense to me.

Finn took a couple steps up to the pop-out counter. He was so confused he didn't know whether to scratch his fancy watch or wind his ass.

I stepped up to the window.

"What'llyahave?" Jolee's words strung together, leaving Finn with a dazed look. Her smile grew with each chomp of her gum. Her blond hair was just long enough to be parted into pigtails that dangled right past her cheek. The freckles that dotted the bridge of her nose made it look like she had a nice bronze tan all year round.

His mouth hung slightly open, his brows furrowed.

"Well?" I shrugged.

"Excuse me." Finn leaned a little closer. "What did you say?"

"To eat?" Jolee jerked her head back. "Where you from?"

"Chicago," I said before he had time to answer.

"Oh. A Yank." She took a couple good chomps of her gum, moving it from one side to the other. "I suggest the Kentucky hot brown sandwich. A little oozy, but a whole lot of goodness." She shifted to the side and planted her hand on her bony hip, waiting for Finn to agree with her.

"I'll just have a plain turkey on white, thank you."

"Yankee," Jolee scoffed and turned her back on us.

"Aren't you ordering?" he asked.

"She knows what I want." I waited patiently but my taste buds were already oozing.

"Sunny Goose Sammy for you." Jolee put my usual in a paper carton on top of the counter, a cup of coffee next to it. "And a Yankee sandwich for you." She sat Finn's plain turkey sandwich next to mine.

"Pepsi?" Finn asked.

"You didn't order a Coke." Jolee was getting a little feisty.

"Right, I'm ordering a Pepsi..." he said, trying to figure her out.

"Well." She straightened her shoulders and twirled one of her pigtails with her finger. "When you ask nicely." She grinned back. "One problem, we only serve Coke."

"That's fine," Finn stuttered, not knowing how to handle Jolee.

"Every little thing..." The sounds of an acoustic guitar and a low almost-whisper of a voice sang the late great Bob Marley's song. Very fitting for the community at this time.

Finn pulled a dollar out of his pocket when we walked by the guitarist and glanced around. "Where's his tip jar?" he asked. His eyes held a sheen of purpose.

"Oh, he doesn't take tips." I nodded over to the steps leading up to Lulu's Boutique craft room. "He just plays around town to get in practice for his band."

"Huh." Finn's brows crossed.

I ordered Duke not to move away from the door. Who was I kidding? The dog did what he wanted. Everyone in town knew him, so if he did meander off, he'd be fine.

We walked inside the craft room where there were only two small tables that weren't taken.

"You weren't kidding when you said Jolee came up with a great idea." Finn looked around the room. The aroma of Jolee's home-cooking swirled into the air.

"We are eating high on the hog now." My mouth watered because I knew what I was about to eat.

"How about over there?" His head flung in the direction of a table in the back corner of the room next to the shelf of unopened yarns.

We weaved our way in and out of the filled chairs. I tried not to make eye contact with too many people, knowing if I did they would ask me about Doc Walton.

When we sat down, Finn set the files between us and grabbed his sandwich, taking a big bite out of it.

I tapped the files. "We can just divide them in half. You take the first half and I'll take the second."

He nodded and kept eating.

I took a bite of my sandwich and sat it back in the carton. I thumbed through the stack. There were names I recognized. Names that weren't alarming or had any reason to kill Doc Walton. My eyes scanned down the tabs of the files. It was going to take a while to go and see all these people. Surely there was an answer to who the killer was in this stack.

"Calling all units! Calling all units!" Betty's shrill voice made me jump as it shrieked over the walkie-talkie. Immediately I scrolled the volume button down, making Betty's voice come through as a whisper.

"What the hell is that?" Finn jerked up, looking at me as if I had two heads. His eyes drew to the walkie-talkie.

"My radio." I patted it and tilted my ear to my shoulder.

"It's a walkie-talkie. Is that what you use to communicate with dispatch?" he asked.

I nodded, trying to listen to him and Betty at the same time.

"You need to look into the earpieces that are less bulky and where no one can hear the dispatcher." Finn looked over both of his shoulders. I looked too. He was right. Everyone in the room had stopped talking and eating, all eyes on me.

"Kenni, robbery in progress at White's Jewelry. Polly Parker called." Betty didn't even wait until I responded to her calling-all-units plea.

"Grab the files." I jumped up and scooped up my food. A fancy new earpiece would have to wait. "We've got to go."

I waved toward Jolee on my way to my Jeep and pointed at Duke. It was our universal signal for her to take him home for me during her Meals On Wheels run. She gave the thumbs up and called him over.

I jumped in the Jeep, licked the suction cup on the old beacon, stuck it on top of the roof, and flipped on the siren.

Chapter Four

The outside of the jewelry store looked as it did every day. The gray awning above the double doors of the shop flapped in the light breeze. "White's Jewelry" was written in calligraphy across the front windows of the shop with two solitaire diamond outlines on each side.

"It doesn't look like a break-in from out here," Finn noted and walked the perimeter of the building. "I'll go secure the back," he said and I agreed, heading inside.

"Thank God you're here." Polly Parker threw her hands up in the air. She stood behind the shattered glass counter.

"Did you check the back?" I asked, my hand on the holster. The shop needed to be secured, but I didn't want to alarm Polly.

"Of course I did." Polly rolled her eyes and stuck her hand on her hips.

"You stay right there and don't move." I walked around the counter. I noticed a crowbar on the floor. I stepped over it and walked to the cracked door behind Polly, using the toe of my boot to push it open. The light was on. The room had jewelry cleaning equipment, some tools for making jewelry, and a door that led out to the alleyway.

"I told you nothing was back there," Polly huffed. She jumped when someone pounded on the back room door.

"Sheriff," Finn called from behind the closed door.

I walked over and let him in.

"Everything looks fine from around and behind the building. It's all secure." He walked up front with me.

"I'm going to question Polly. You walk around the shop and see if you notice anything out of place." I unzipped my bag and took out the tape recorder. "There's a crowbar next to the busted-up counter, which I assume is what was used to shatter the glass."

"I'll see if there are any prints and gather it for evidence." Finn went straight to the crowbar and bent down.

"Who are you?" Polly's little button nose curled, her body shifting toward Finn.

"He's with the reserves." My eyes drifted to the cloth around his neck.

There was no sense in going into the details of who Finn was. Most of the time the reserves would send someone, but it wasn't unusual for them to get switched in the middle of investigations.

I sat a tape recorder on the glass counter of White's Jewelry right in front of Polly Parker and pressed the record button.

"Tell me exactly what happened." I took out my pad of paper and a pen.

Polly was suddenly visibly shaken up when I asked her the question. Much different than a moment ago. She wrung her petite hands together, her diamonds clicking against each other as each finger rolled over the top of them.

"Is this on?" Polly leaned over the tape recorder. The edges of her chopped blond hair dangled in a perfect line.

"Yes. It is." I tried to give her an encouraging smile. "Can you tell me what happened?"

"Sonofabitch thought he was going to get away with it." It was like she suddenly had an audience. Her perfectly lined pink pouty mouth contorted, her nose snarled, and she spat between her veneers I was sure were stuck in her small mouth by Dr. Beverly—Bev for short—Houston.

I was no dentist by any stretch of the imagination, but I knew veneers weren't supposed to make your mouth resemble that of a horse, which Polly's did. Her teeth were too big for her five-foot-two-inch, one-hundred-pound frame and small face. But she didn't care. She yammered on and on about how she wasn't going to let the thief get away and she was sure it was one of the new seedy residents at the new condominium complex overlooking the river.

"Probably robbed Doc Walton thinking he had a lot of money since he was an old doctor and all," she rambled, making sure she spoke as close to the tape recorder as possible without putting her lips on it. "But when he didn't have nothing to give, I bet they shanked him and decided to come where there was money for sure." Her bloodshot eyes slid up, catching mine for a split second. "Toots." She gasped, putting her hand up over her mouth. "Is Toots okay?" she asked about her best friend. "Did the killer get her?" Her head bobbed up and down like one of those bobble-heads. Her blue eyes didn't blink once. The pearls around her neck didn't move, distracting me; I couldn't figure out for the life of me how they stayed still with each bobble. She waved her hand back and forth, her wrist missing the pearl bracelet with the monogrammed circle charm she always wore.

"Toots is fine," I assured her. I got back to writing down the main points of her day, and starting with the first one sounded like a pretty good idea. "Tell me exactly what you saw when you first unlocked the door."

"Oh my stars, Kenni Lowry. I told you everything already. Did you not get it?" She tried to close her lips around those big teeth. "Don't tell me my daddy is right about you and this job, because I have paid all hell for two years for voting for you. And your mama and daddy are just beside themselves. My daddy said he would take himself to his own grave if I ever took a job as a sheriff. A man's job." She crossed her arms.

Keep calm, keep calm. That voice drifted past me.

"Are you okay?" Polly asked.

I blinked a few times, a fake grin across my face, trying to keep my crazy at bay. "I understand you are upset and you have been violated." I decided to listen to my conscience and keep calm.

Polly was such a pretty princess daddy's girl that she was used to being coddled and handled with kid gloves even though she was only one year younger than me.

"But I have to know every single detail. Please take your time and try to remember everything." I looked down at my pad of paper and tried to put the voice in the back of my head.

"I told you I bet it's the same man who killed Doc Walton." Her voice escalated to a high-pitch twang with a little bit of a whine. "But this looks just like something that would come out of that seedy place." She pointed to the ground behind the counter.

I walked around and looked at the symbol spray-painted on the tight-threaded tan carpet.

"That's some sort of graffiti shit you see in a big city, and I bet some of those hoodlums in those condos did it. Damn Doolittle Bowman." Polly spat ugly words out of her pretty mouth when she cursed Cottonwood's town council president for pushing the vote through to build condominiums.

I took my camera out of my bag and took a couple of pictures of the symbol on the carpet. It reminded me of Chinese writing, which I knew nothing about, but I bet my good buddy Google would.

"Please do not go spreading rumors about the condominium owners. There is no evidence anyone living there has anything to do with this crime." I took pictures from all angles. "Where is your bracelet?"

There was an uncomfortable silence between us.

"I..." She rubbed her hand on her wrist. "I had taken it off here so I could clean it." Her head jerked around. Her eyes darted about. "Oh my God! They stole my bracelet. I left it right there." She pointed to the cleaning cloth on top of the counter. "I was going to finish cleaning it today."

"Hello?" a voice called from the front door of the jewelry store. I reached over and clicked off the tape recorder.

"Mayor!" Polly jumped up and ran around the counter, throwing her hands around Mayor Chance Ryland's waist, letting out a big sob. "Kenni has lost her cotton pickin' mind."

"Now, now." Chance rubbed a flat palm down Polly's back. "Your daddy is on the way to come get you and take you home."

The mayor and Pete Parker had been long time friends. To my understanding Mayor Ryland was like an uncle to Polly, but my uncle never patted me like that. There was a rumor running around the women's social circles about an affair between the two. My ick factor shot up just thinking about it. But I'd thought it was just a rumor, like most small-town gossip.

Mayor Ryland was debonair and fit for a man in his sixties. His black hair was slicked back, his strong jaw tensed. When he started running, dying his hair black, and growing the goatee along with a lot of manscaping, the rumor started that he was sleeping with Polly Parker. Seeing them firsthand, clinging together, I wouldn't doubt it.

"Thank you for your interest, Mayor, but if you don't mind stepping outside, this is a crime scene." I spoke in a calm, matter-of-fact tone. "And when Pete gets here, you can tell him we will send Polly out when we are finished questioning her."

"Kenni, surely you can understand Polly has been through an ordeal here." Chance's hand moved slowly up and down Polly's back.

Finn, who'd been quietly observing while I questioned Polly, looked at me. Our eyes met with amusement. I was used to the small-town politics and how people protected their own at any level.

"I guess you need to listen to Sheriff Lowry." He let go of Polly, giving her a "be a good girl" nod before slamming the front door of White's behind him.

"I'm going to go in the back and see if anything jumps out at me." Finn stepped in the back room.

I waited a few seconds to collect my thoughts and take a few deep breaths before I continued my line of questioning with Polly.

"Why were you here today?" I asked. Polly didn't own the place, Viola White did, and Viola was rarely one to miss a day at the store.

"I'm filling in for Mrs. White because she has a terrible head cold." The southern charm dripped out of Polly's mouth like honey.

Polly bit the corner of her mouth. She shook her finger at me. "Mrs. White said she'd gone to see if she could get an appointment with Doc Walton, which was how I found out about Doc Walton, you know." She ran her skinny finger across her neck.

I was not entertained. "Keep going," I said flatly.

"There were no visible signs of a break-in, so I entered. I had to even use my key." She gestured to the counter. "Then I came in to put my purse up and saw this." She pointed to the broken cases and the floor with the spray-painted mural.

"Just like the movies." Polly sighed slowly. "Then I immediately called 911."

"You didn't see a robber?" I asked. Mr. Parker parked his fancy Cadillac in front of the jewelry store in a handicap spot. I held back on giving him a ticket. The Parkers always thought they were above the law and that always bothered me.

If I recalled from Betty's distress call, she had said it was a robbery in progress.

"No." Slowly she shook her head, bob not moving. "Still, it's not every day a murder and a robbery occur in Cottonwood. Hell," she cackled, "it's not every year. Every other year." She made it sound much worse each time she opened her mouth.

"You can go. Don't be surprised if I have you come down to the station for some more questions."

"Well, Kenni Lowry, if I didn't know better, I'd think you think I did this," she snarled. Her eyes lowered, glaring at me, but quickly shot up when she looked at Finn, who had come back into the room a few minutes ago. Her nose even uncurled, allowing her lips to part in a big grin, exposing those damn veneers. She walked out the door.

"She's a wild card." Finn's voice held an entertained tone. "She's something."

"Polly is something all right. Don't get me started." I bit back my true feelings for her. Hillbilly with money. Daddy's money. Her odd behavior as a victim really set my internal radar off. She wasn't there when the theft occurred. And she wasn't held hostage or even saw a gun. I made a mental note to watch her behavior. I wasn't so sure she didn't have something to do with this. I didn't have a connection, but something felt off.

"What in the hell is around your neck?" I asked Finn, keeping my observations about Polly to myself.

"Your mom's scarf from Lulu. She gave it to me after you jumped in line at the food truck and told me to give it to you." He rubbed down it. "You don't think I look good?"

"Take it off," I ordered, rolling my eyes.

"Lulu wouldn't let me leave without it." He uncurled the uneven scarf from around his neck. "I'd keep it, but it's not my initials," Finn joked, lessening the tension around us.

"Funny." I grabbed the scarf from his grip. "It's not nice to make fun of people. Ms. Lulu probably worked really hard on this scarf."

I wasn't about to tell him that she was really trying to work hard on repairing my relationship with my mother. A relationship that wasn't going to be repaired until I decided not to be sheriff.

"You know..." He paused, holding the scarf out between us in a taunting way. When I went to grab it, he hoisted it up in the air away from my hands. "You should probably go see your mom."

"Got it!" I grabbed the free dangling end and tugged. I tugged again, realizing he wasn't going to let go. My eyes slid up his arm, along his shoulder, along his neckline, and found his eyes. His suit jacket was snug around his arm, taut around the seam where the sleeve met the shoulder. I tossed the idea around of what he might look like under the suit, then shook myself back to the conversation. So much for not telling him about the real reason Lulu wanted me to take the scarf to my mom.

"My mama is not part of an investigation or a crime." I jerked the scarf, forced to take a few steps backward when he released it, and tried not to land on my hinny.

"It's sort of a crime not to talk to the only mother you have." He crossed his arms and parted his legs in that stance the TV cops always did.

"You know what..." I wasn't about to tell this stranger my problems. They had nothing to do with the death of Doc Walton or the break-in at White's Jewelry. "Let's stick with catching the bad guys."

"Guys?" he questioned me.

"Yeah. Guys."

"What makes you think it's guys and not girls?"

"What?" A scowl crossed my face and I tried to erase it, but I couldn't. It was one of those moments when your mama tells you that if you make that face it will freeze that way. Well, mine just might have frozen.

"What makes you so sure guys did this?" he asked. "If you think about it, Doc Walton has several stab wounds that really didn't make any sense. They were all over. Plus, I'm not so sure it was an actual knife that was used as the weapon. And I've been around enough crime scenes to know he probably laid there and bled out from his wounds. The stab wounds weren't deep. Just very many. Which makes me believe..." Finn did a lot of stabbing motions in the air. "The killer was provoked by something they were talking about and she grabbed something sharp and began stabbing him, maybe not strong enough to penetrate deep."

"Good point." I threw the scarf back on his shoulder.

I wasn't going to discount what Finn was saying, nor was I going to agree with it all. As far as I knew, Doc Walton didn't have any enemies and had no reason for someone to kill him. And this wasn't some big city where strange and unusual ways of killing someone occurred.

Chapter Five

"Don't tell me you are lollygagging around here and not finding my jewelry." Viola White ripped the police tape in front of the propped open door and waltzed right on in, blue feathers flying behind her. "Because me and the good people I begged to vote for you didn't vote you in so you could lollygag."

Viola might have been five foot four, but her presence was larger than life. Finn Vincent knew it. He had his eyes wide open and mouth gaping trying to take in the compact bomb in the light blue pantsuit. Viola was by far the richest woman in Cottonwood, as well as the most eccentric.

Her suit coat edges were trimmed in the blue feathers. Thank God PETA didn't know about her or they'd be stalking her. Viola wore a lot of fur, feathers, quills, and other animal parts that made my skin crawl, but she didn't care.

The baseball-sized turquoise beads around her neck intertwined with six more strands of various-sized beads and matching bracelets along her arm.

"Lollygagging?" Finn's lips turned up and a sparkle came into his eyes. "Cottonwood has very colorful residents."

"I appreciate all you did to help get me elected." I rocked back on the heels of my shoes. "And I'm going to find out who did this."

"Yes." Finn stuck his hand out. "I'm Finn Vincent. I'll be assisting Sheriff Lowry with this investigation."

Viola White had known me all my life. She was a friend of my granny and Poppa.

"Where'd you get that?" Viola didn't care about personal space. She jerked the scarf off of Finn's shoulder.

"Miss Lulu." Finn smiled. I could tell he was trying to figure out what Viola White was all about.

"Lulu?" Viola harrumphed, flapping her bright red lips.

She ruffled the edges of her short gray hair with her pointer finger and middle finger. A big turquoise ring stuck up in the air along with her pinky finger. Her heavily mascaraed eyes looked magnified beneath her coffee-cup-sized black-rimmed glasses.

I couldn't help but grin. Viola wouldn't be caught dead out in public without makeup.

"Heavens to Betsy, if you are going to stay around Cottonwood, you need to know that Lulu McClain is crookeder than a three-dollar bill." Viola's nose turned up and she moseyed over to the broken counter. "Butter wouldn't melt in her mouth."

I listened to her give Finn the business. He looked so lost. He had no idea that he had just been what we called "Viola'd." She was good at giving a tongue lashing and hugging you afterward.

"Ma'am, with all due respect," Finn began, but Viola quickly threw up her finger and wagged it in his face. "Please don't touch anything as this is a crime scene," he finished.

I bit my lip. He was about to get Viola'd again.

"Listen here, all due respect to you, but Polly called me in a tizzy. That is the only girl in town I trust with my jewels and I'll be damned if this gets put on the back burner to Ronald Walton." Viola didn't miss a beat, barely taking a breath between sentences. Her lips pursed. "Who ever heard of a doctor's office being in a house?" She turned to me and took her wagging finger out of the air and jutted it toward me. "Kenni, when you took away his driver's license, you should've taken away his doctoring license too." Viola's eyes scanned over the broken glass all over the floor.

"Ma'am, that would be the job of the Medical Board," Finn said. He glowed as he took pride in trying to converse with Viola, but I knew better.

"Around here we use the town council board to decide what is best for Cottonwood." The bracelets on her wrists clinked together when she planted her fists on her hips, and they disappeared behind all the feathers. "The quicker you figure that out, the quicker people around here will like you, Yank. Looks can only get you so far around here, sonny boy."

Finn and I stood silent, neither of us daring to move as Viola walked around the broken glass. She was writing away on a piece of paper she'd plucked from her purse.

I'd heard about Viola's tongue lashings but never been present for one. They were as awful as I'd heard, and Finn was the victim today. It would be all over town as soon as Viola went to her prayer circle meeting down at First Baptist Church.

"Well, what are you waiting for?" She circled her finger around the crime scene. She handed me the piece of paper. "You better hurry up because we are burning daylight and I want my jewels back by tonight," Viola demanded before she stomped over to the door. "And Kenni..."

"Yes, ma'am."

My voice sounded like a little girl's. I looked at what she'd written on the paper. The jewels were listed with a price next to each one.

"You be a good girl and take that scarf over to your mama and daddy's." Her face was stern. "You solve these crimes and show them that you are a good sheriff. They'll come around."

"Thank you for caring about my personal life. How are you feeling?" I asked. I knew Viola was a patient of Doc Walton's and Polly Parker did say she was here because Viola had a head cold.

Her voice wasn't nasally nor was her face blotchy, or did those symptoms only happen to me?

"I'm fine." She took her hands and ran them down the lining around her neck. Feathers went flying. "Are you trying to put me at the scene of Ronald's house? Are you thinking I broke into my own store?"

It did cross my mind that Viola could have broken in. I'd overheard some woman at Euchre talking about a rumor that

White's was closing down due to low sales. I couldn't discount that there might've been some insurance money somewhere.

"Polly said she was here because you had a head cold." I smiled, waiting to see her reaction.

"I'm better." She straightened her shoulders and stomped out onto Main Street.

Chapter Six

"What was that about?" Finn asked, tossing me the scarf. He cocked his head to the side in curiosity.

"I've seen Viola White sick with a cold." I pointed out the door where she was jerking her head back and forth, talking to the small crowd that had gathered on the other side of the broken police tape. "And she doesn't look sick to me."

"Are you really saying you think she had something to do with this?" he asked, scratching his chin. "Not that it couldn't happen."

"Think about it." I started to play the "what if" game, deciding to leave out the fact that I was going off gossip alone. "Viola is used to living a certain life around here. Being the wealthiest woman has its advantages."

He snapped his fingers. "And I'm sure she had a nice insurance policy."

"I'm sure she did." I grinned and grabbed the pad of paper and a pen out of my bag. I scribbled a reminder to ask Hart Insurance about any policy Viola might have on the business.

"I have to run, but can you just scour this place one more time for fingerprints, clues, and anything else you see out of place?" I asked, gathering my stuff.

I left Finn at White's Jewelry to look for any signs of forced entry since there was nothing visible. I decided to make a pit stop by the cemetery, which was on Main Street down a block or two from the jewelry store and across from Ben's, the oh-so-original name for Ben Harrison's diner.

A few people were walking down the sidewalk and stopped to

wave at me as I passed. The looks on their faces seemed curious about where I was going in case there was another crime. At least that was what I saw in their eyes.

The old cemetery was the only public one in Cottonwood. The big cement urns were popping with yellow, purple, orange, and white flowers.

Not everyone who died was buried in the cemetery. Some residents had family cemeteries on their property. Just a few blocks south of Main Street was Second Street, or the Town Branch as we affectionately called it, because a small creek bed, sometimes wet but mostly dry, ran right through the entire length of town. Second Street had a lot of old Victorian homes that were built in the twenties. Back then people buried family members on their property.

I took a right on Cemetery Road into the old cemetery and stopped to see what some of the city workers were doing along the slave wall that surrounded the area. The large stonewalls were all over Kentucky. They were built by slaves, and by state law, had to be kept up and preserved. That was what it looked like they were doing today.

"Mornin', Sheriff," Rowdy Hart hollered out and waved. His expanding gut tumbled over the top of his pants. It was a shame too. Rowdy had always been in such good shape.

"Hey, Rowdy." I waved out of the window of the truck.

The old truck groaned around the curvy one-lane road that weaved in and around the gravestones. Some of the stones were so old mold had grown up over them. Recently the city had opened up a couple of acres in the back of the property for new plots and from what I'd heard, people were buying them up before they were even dead.

Today I was going to the older part, where I was a frequent visitor. I pulled the passenger-side tires into the grass and kept the driver-side tires on the road, pulling over to stop right in front of the grave and leaving enough room for other cars to drive by.

I peered out the passenger-side window and stared at the

three-foot-tall typical cement gravestone. I pushed the steering wheel gear shifter into park and took out the keys, dropping them on the floorboard.

"Ugh." I sighed and looked between my legs, scraping my foot on the floorboard to help kick them back toward me, but like everything else today, they weren't cooperating with me either.

I opened the door and bent down into the truck.

"Where in the hell did they go?" I questioned, as if someone was going to answer me.

I patted my hand underneath the seat and jerked it out when I felt something stick me.

"Shit!" I put my bleeding finger in my mouth to stop the blood, and then took it out to inspect where something had poked me. "Damn," I said, looking at it closer and pinching it, causing the blood to come out in little drops.

I grabbed the flashlight out of my handy dandy bag and bent back down, shining it under the seat, where I found my keys and a little lapel pin next to them. I raked both of them forward, careful not to poke myself again. I put the keys in my pocket and held the pin in the palm of my hand while taking a look at it from all angles.

I smiled.

It was my Poppa's pin from when he was Cottonwood sheriff, though I wondered why they hadn't buried it with him. After all, he was buried in his uniform.

"Somehow you knew I was coming." I took a step forward, an inch closer toward the most important man from my past. I put the pin in my pocket. I ran my hand along the top of the stone and cleared off any loose debris. "There is something strange going on around here, and I'm not so sure I'm going to win this one."

Tears stung the rims of my eyes at the sheer thought of Poppa being gone. One day he was here, healthy as a bull, and then the next day I found him next to his bed, dead of a heart attack. People say time healed all wounds; I wondered when my time was going to start. My heart was just as broken now as it had been when he died.

"I'm so scared that I'm not going to be able to put all the

puzzle pieces together to solve these crimes." I plopped down crossed-legged in front of Poppa's stone like I was plopping down on his sofa as I'd done so many times before and kept talking. "I sure do wish you were here to help."

In some strange way it did make me feel better to visit Poppa's final resting place. Sometimes I walked away with answers to the questions I was fighting within me.

"I don't know where to start. Doc Walton has been murdered. Someone broke into White's Jewelry." I wiped my face with the palm of my hand. "None of this ever happened when you were sheriff." I put my head in my hands.

I remembered the pin and pulled it out of my front pocket. I sobbed. "I found this pin in the truck today. And Wyatt said something about the old police beacon light and how I still use it. I guess he was right." I picked up a blade of grass and twirled it between my fingers. "I'm going to make you proud. I'm going to figure out who killed Doc and who broke into the jewelry store."

"Kenni, you alright?" Rowdy asked from behind me.

I jumped up, wiping my face and turning toward him.

"Rowdy, are you sneaking up on me?" I asked. He looked at me cross. "Sure, I'm fine." I waved off the real concern he had written all over his face. "Why?" I couldn't tell if Rowdy was fishing for information about the two open investigations or if he was just being kind. He wasn't the nosy type, so I was going with kindness. It was something I needed to believe in.

"Aw, I don't know." He bent down and plucked a couple weeds out of the grass. "It's just that I've seen you here quite a bit lately." He pointed to Poppa's stone.

"I'm fine." I laughed and walked past him. "Are you okay?" I asked, taking the heat off of me.

"Just tired." He ran his hands through his curly brown hair. "I've been out at the fairgrounds all night making sure the drainage was working." He shook his head. "I told Mayor Ryland he might have to postpone it."

"I don't think the mayor would like that." There was no way

Chance Ryland was going to postpone anything that made Cottonwood money. I took the first steps back to the truck. I had to get out of there.

Stop loafing. You have a job to do. The whisper was a tad bit louder.

I swallowed hard. I gritted my teeth. Shuffling my feet, I did the best I could to ignore the voice in my head. I picked up the pace.

"It would be safer for the town if he did." Rowdy trotted alongside me. "There is no way the carnival is going to put up rides in that mud puddle out there. It just wouldn't be safe."

"I've got a few cases to solve," I called over my shoulder, now with another thing to worry about on my mind. I was going to have to check out the fairgrounds and make an assessment of the situation, and possibly make a doctor's appointment to check my head.

I raised my hand in the air. "Bye," I hollered.

Jerking the keys out of my pocket, I jumped into the truck and jabbed them in the ignition, dropping them back on the ground along with the pin. "Damn!" I grabbed my palm, bleeding from another pin stick.

Nothing was going right today. Nothing.

I pushed in the walkie-talkie and said, "Betty."

Pulling out of the cemetery, I took a right on Main Street. I really wanted to please Viola, but Doc Walton's murder was more important on the list of crimes.

"Betty," I yelled, thinking she didn't hear me the first time.

"Kenni, I'm here," she snapped, sounding out of breath. "You wouldn't believe all the calls we're getting. And people stopping in to get information."

Oh yes I would. I shook my head. She continued talking and I heard some whispering in the background.

"They are all curious to know if you have any leads on the murder and the break-in. And if the seedy condos by Doc's house are where it all started?" Betty asked.

"Betty, you can tell everyone that's hanging around Cowboy's and drinking coffee that I do not discuss official business. They should go home." If I stayed on the walkie-talkie any longer, I just might lose it. "Can you please call Wyatt and ask him to drive out to the fairgrounds and check to make sure there's no flooding?"

"Sure can, Ken—" She stopped herself. "Sheriff Lowry."

"Oh, I'd almost forgotten, I need you to call the mayor. I'd like them to call an emergency meeting as soon as they can get it scheduled."

"Kenni." Betty stopped me from hanging up. "I mean, Sheriff, Max Bogus just called. He said he had something to show you, so you need to stop by the funeral home."

Chapter Seven

Max Bogus's hearse was parked next to the funeral home. I pulled up behind him and parked the Jeep. The lapel pin was still in my grasp. My heart took a dip when I looked at the pin and could clearly remember Poppa wearing it. I stuck it through my shirt. In my bag was a pencil; I popped off the eraser and used it as a stopper to keep the pin in place.

The morgue and funeral home was a one-stop shop. Like any business in Cottonwood, the door to the funeral home was unlocked and I let myself in. There wasn't any commotion coming from the funeral home and Max's hearse was outside, which meant one thing: I was going to have to go downstairs to the morgue to find Max.

I stood in the doorway, my eyes fixed on naked Doc Walton. Though it was almost lunch, it was still too early to see a corpse, much less that of Doc Walton.

"You aren't going to believe what I found on Ronald." Max and Doc Walton had been friends. "It's the strangest thing."

"What?"

Max stood over Doc with a scalpel in his hand, blue lab coat slung open, a big pair of goggles on his round face. He looked up. His black eyes were round like large marbles. "Don't tell me you're squeamish."

"No, not at all." I gulped, taking a step closer.

Suddenly, as if someone was pushing me from behind, my feet scooted across the floor without me picking them up.

"Did you see..." I jumped around and pointed to the door and then back to where I was standing. "Was someone..."

I wanted to ask if he had seen someone behind me, but I knew no one else was there. I closed my eyes and took a deep breath. Seeing Doc Walton's corpse was playing a number on my senses.

"Are you okay?" Max glanced over Doc Walton at me.

"I'm fine." I turned to the metal tray table next to me and grabbed a couple of gloves from the box.

"Some people aren't good around dead people. Trust me, it's not only you." Max's voice was calming.

I turned back around and gave him a kind smile.

"I'm fine." I forced my eyes down to the corpse. "Now, tell me what you discovered."

"This." He turned over Doc's wrist, where there was some sort of tattoo.

"Who knew he was such a rebel?" I tried to make a joke out of it, not successfully.

"It's not a tat. It's Sharpie marker. On his right wrist." He used a pointer to point to Doc's other hand. "Ronald has never been able to write properly with his left hand, nor deal a good hand in poker, because the tip is gone off the pointer finger. He was right-handed." He dragged the pointer over to the Sharpie design. "This is intricate detail Ronald could've never done with his left hand. Plus, when I swipe it, parts of it rub off easily because it's not been there long."

The design written in Sharpie on Doc's wrist reminded me of something. Then it hit me like a ton of bricks.

White's Jewelry, I thought to myself.

"White's Jewelry," a soft and gentle voice spoke back.

My head shifted side to side. "I'm sorry." I leaned a little over Doc's body. "Did you say White's Jewelry?"

"No." Max's brows furrowed. "I said there is no way—"

"Yeah, yeah." I waved him off. "I heard you say that, but you didn't say anything about the jewelry store? And the break-in?"

"No."

"You don't know." I gasped. "You've been down here all

morning." I gestured to the autopsy room. "White's Jewelry was broken into before Polly Parker opened up for Viola White and this exact same symbol was spray-painted on the carpet behind the glass counter."

Somehow Doc Walton's murder and the White's Jewelry theft were related, and the killer wanted me to know.

"I even took pictures of it but I left my bag out in the truck." I held a finger up. "I'll be right back."

A clear glass jar full of Band-Aids was sitting on the counter on my way out of the autopsy. I lifted the lid off.

"You don't mind if I use one, do you?" I asked, peeling the gloves off of my hands.

"No, take what you need." Max was bent over with a magnifier stuck on his goggles taking a good look at the Sharpie tattoo.

Walking out to the truck, I ripped the Band-Aid open and made it tight around my finger like my mother used to do when I was a child. Oh, how I missed those days.

Follow your instincts. The whisper filled my head. My heart sank and I took a few quick breaths.

I grabbed my bag, taking it back inside.

"I swear it's the same symbol from White's," I said as I rushed back into the autopsy room, where Max was still hunkered over the corpse.

I sat my bag on the counter, deliberately keeping my back turned, not facing the procedure until I heard some clicking noises.

"What are you doing?" I asked, looking at Max, who was holding a fancy digital SLR camera.

His hand was placed on the lens, rotating it left and right, clicking with the other. He would squat, stand, and move around the body like he was a photographer on the set of *America's Next Top Model* and Doc Walton was the model.

"I have to take pictures of everything." He didn't miss an angle. His finger continued to snap away. "It's part of the procedure. Especially in a murder investigation."

It might be sick, but for the first time today, I felt a little better.

Taking any more pictures myself than I needed to of Doc Walton's dead body was not high on my priority list. I wasn't looking forward to downloading them at home tonight as I stirred my spaghetti.

"I had to take pictures while Ronald was in the body bag." His voice cracked, and I looked over at him. There were tears in his eyes. He cleared his throat. "And when I transferred him to the table."

I walked over and put my hand on his shoulder. He continued to snap.

"I'm sorry." I wasn't sure how to console him. "I know y'all were poker buddies and friends."

He stepped away from my hand, putting the camera down on the stainless steel table next to Doc Walton, and peeled off his gloves, the bags under his eyes damp.

"I've never had to do an autopsy on a friend before." He nodded for me to follow him. He picked his camera up, putting the strap around his neck. He lowered the exam table, grabbed his camera, and took pictures of Doc's face. "What in the world?" He let the camera dangle and grabbed a pair of tweezers.

"What?" The shock in his voice had me hoping it was something important.

"Is this mercury from a thermometer?" He held the tweezers under the magnifying lens.

"There was a broken thermometer on the floor. Doc Walton didn't believe in the battery ones." I thought about going to see him as a child and having to put that glass thermometer in my mouth for what seemed like a long time. I almost smiled.

"I know, but why was this embedded in his mustache?" Max asked.

"Embedded?" I asked and leaned over Doc Walton's face.

Max used the tips of the tweezers to rake through Doc's mustache. "See?" The tweezers parted a couple of hairs to expose another ball of the mercury.

Carefully, Max put the mercury ball into a beaker with the other one.

"You don't think he could have dropped the thermometer while he was being stabbed?" I asked. "Maybe he was taking the killer's temperature. The killer could have taken Doc off guard and stabbed him. Doc dropped the thermometer, breaking it, and the mercury rolled everywhere. When he fell to the ground, he fell face forward into the mercury, getting it in his mustache."

It seemed like a pretty good analysis, if I said so myself.

"There are no cuts on his face." Max grabbed his magnifying glass and looked down through it. "If he landed in glass, he would've had some cuts. Besides, when I moved his body, there wasn't a pile of mercury or glass."

"Oh." I bit my lip, disappointed that my theory was probably wrong.

"Kenni." Max put the magnifying glass down. His tone became chilly. "I think I can guess how Ronald died."

"Guess?" There was no room for guessing.

"I'm pretty sure I know." His voice cracked. "I think the killer somehow made Ronald ingest the mercury."

"What?"

I had never heard of such a thing.

"Ronald might have been stabbed multiple times, but he most likely died from ingested mercury balls." He put his hand over his mouth like he was being smothered. "I believe the balls on the floor fell out of the killer's hand when they were trying to smother Doc. He does have some bruising on the back of his neck, which makes sense if the killer grabbed Doc and forced the mercury balls from the broken thermometer over his mouth and nose. When Doc tried to catch some air, the mercury balls would've slid down his passageways. This would explain the little blood in his mouth, his swollen eyelids, and bloodshot eyes." He moved his hand over every body part he had named that would be affected by the poisoning. "It's hard to trace and the killer was smart enough to know that. And," he moved his finger over one of the stab wounds, "they were very angry with him to keep stabbing him."

"So your theory is the killer stabbed him first and saw it wasn't going to do the job so they broke the thermometer, got out the mercury globules, and forced them down Doc's throat?" I asked.

"I'm just here to figure out how he died." Max motioned for me to follow him to his office. He talked into a mini tape recorder, reciting exactly what he had told me. "I have to put in all theories to help me put the facts together. Ronald will tell me how he died."

"Ronald will what?"

"His body will tell me how he was killed," Max spat. This was the first time I had heard him sound angry.

We walked into his office right off of the autopsy room. The room was bare. There were two chairs in front of his desk, neither of them matching, which made me think they came from Ruby's Antiques on Main Street. Behind the desk was a bookshelf wall, only it didn't hold a single book. It was filled with files upon files.

"Have a seat." Max took a seat in the chair behind the desk. "I have to find out what happened in Ronald's office last night."

"Me too." He had to know how serious I was. "Last night?"

"The wound marks can tell me a lot." He flipped his fancy camera on and showed me a picture of some of the wounds.

"What is that?" I asked, pointing to the stuff around the wound.

"It's Steri-Strips. Like Band-Aids. They help me take a good picture of each wound so I can measure the depth and figure out the mapping." He flipped to the next picture. "If the blood tests come back toxic with mercury, I'll be able to use the mapping to figure out if he was stabbed first, and when that didn't do the job, they used the mercury."

"How does the mapping work?" I asked.

He put the camera down and took in a deep breath. I could tell he was a little frustrated with my lack of knowledge. "I can determine by the pattern of the wounds how and in what order they were created. I'm wondering if the killer didn't intend to kill him, but something set them off and they killed him on impulse. That might explain the random pattern of stabbings." He drew his arm up over his head, pointing to his shoulder blade. "The x-rays show the depth of the wounds, and I really have to rule out the stab wounds as the cause of death."

He picked up the x-ray film off his desk. "This shows the stab wounds didn't go into the body enough to hit an organ or any sort of major artery, so I'm deducing the weapon was not a knife."

I stood up and took a closer look.

"These stab wounds look post-mortem." He used his pen to point to the ones he was talking about.

"So Doc was already dead when he was stabbed?"

"Yes, so mercury poisoning is the most likely cause of death." He pointed to more of the post-mortem wounds. "The person who did this must have been very angry. I don't know anyone who would continue to stab someone who was dead unless there was so much hate built up in them that it was the only way to get out their rage."

"Who could have hated him that much?" I thought about who Doc Walton hung out with, and no one fit the profile Max was talking about.

"The preliminary toxicology test will give us some direction." He picked up his camera again and showed me another picture. "His wrist. This symbol was also at the White's Jewelry break-in?"

"Yes." I pulled my camera out of the bag and showed him the pictures of the symbol. "Which leads me to believe the two crimes are connected."

"It looks like some sort of Chinese symbol like you see down at Kim's Buffet." He stared down his nose at me before he took off his reader glasses, setting them aside and folding his hands in front of him on the folders. "You know, I never saw your Poppa a day without that pin on him." His chair creaked when he eased back, crossing his arms over his chest. "He even wore it in church."

I ran my finger over the pin. Mrs. Kim would know what the symbols mean. I needed an expert and she was Chinese. I couldn't get a better expert. "Listen, you keep working on the autopsy and I'm going to figure out this symbol." I jumped up, gathering my stuff before zipping my bag. "I think that's a good place to start."

Chapter Eight

"Kenni, hi!" Ruby Smith waved at me from across the street. Her short red hair sparkled in the early morning sunshine. Her orange-lipstick-lined lips parted, she called, "Wait right there!"

Ruby weaved her long and lanky five-foot-nine frame in and out of Main Street traffic, looking like Frogger in her green jumpsuit, flailing her hands at oncoming traffic to stop and let her pass.

"Use the crosswalk!" someone yelled when they passed her.

Ruby threw her middle finger up and kept going. "I've got a two-for-one special today." She threw both middle fingers up. "People are so rude." She shook her head at me.

"Well, jaywalking is against the law, Ruby." Not that I would give her a citation, but she did need to know she was completely in the wrong when the crosswalk was just a few steps away.

She pushed her wrists toward me, a bag dangling from her grasp.

"Cuff me." Her chin lifted in the air, her eyes sweeping down at me. Her green eyeshadow sparkled. "Take me to jail."

"Ruby." An exhausted sigh escaped me. "I don't have time for this."

"You apparently don't have time to do laundry either." Her lashes whipped up, her eyes as wide as the full moon.

"It's been a long day." I wasn't about to get into a discussion over my attire; I already knew I looked like I had just rolled out of bed.

Which I had this morning, but in my defense, I hadn't planned on seeing anyone, nor investigating a murder or a break-in at White's.

"I just wanted you to know that Viola White called and told me about the robbery." Ruby tucked a loose hair behind her ear. "I called Doolittle Bowman and told her to call an emergency town meeting, but she said someone else had already called in to suggest the same thing." She leaned down and whispered, "And Doc Walton? You need to check out that Doctor Shively." Her painted-on brows arched. "When I went to Ben's for a cup of coffee yesterday, Doc Walton was in there having a heated discussion with Doctor Shively. I wasn't trying to eavesdrop so I didn't hear anything." She gave a theatrical wink. "Toots came into the shop the other day and Doctor Shively was at the register. The two of them avoided each other like the plague. When I asked Toots about it..." She cleared her throat. "Not that I was nosing, but it is my civic duty since I am on the town council."

"Of course you weren't. And of course you are only doing your civic duty." I knew better. Ruby knowing something was as good as putting it in the newspaper. Better, even.

"Toots said Doc Walton and Doctor Shively had seen the same patient and didn't see eye to eye on the patient's treatment." Slowly her head nodded up and down. "I'm sure you'll hear about it at the town council meeting." She wiggled her brows.

The meeting would be like a firing range, only I would be the target and the people of Cottonwood the bullets.

"Thank you for the information about Doc Walton. I'll look into it."

I had to find out what the doctors were fighting about. Why didn't Toots tell me about it?

I held my hand up for a slight wave, and she grabbed it.

"What on earth did you do?" She held my finger up to her eyes and took a good look. "You're bleeding."

"I am?" I jerked my hand out of hers and looked at the Band-Aid.

She was right. The blood trickled down through the Band-Aid and in the creases of my hand.

"Crap." I ran the finger down my shirt.

"Such language," Ruby hissed.

"Really? You just gave someone the bird and you're fussing about the word 'crap?'" I looked at my finger again.

"They were going to hit me." She stomped her foot.

"You were jaywalking." The pin poke continued to let out little dots of blood. I waved her off. "Listen, I was going to come see you because I found a pin of my Poppa's from when he was sheriff."

"He was such a good sheriff." A smile crossed her orange lips. "He would've been all over these crimes. Not that you aren't. Now, what about that pin? I bet it would fetch a pretty penny."

"Oh no." I shook my head and pointed to it on my shirt. "I'm not selling it. I want to wear it on my uniform but I need one of those butterfly clasps to keep it on."

"Darling," Ruby held her bag in the air, "I would say it was your lucky day, but it clearly hasn't been. But I just so happen to have picked up a bunch when I went antiquing yesterday in Clay's Ferry." She opened the bag and put her hand in, pulling out a handful of clasps and extending her palm to me. "I didn't go back to the shop after I found these gems and I was going to put them out today."

Clay's Ferry was another small town known for their antique shops. In order to get there, people had to drive through Cottonwood, which was why Ruby decided to open her shop.

"That is so strange." My head cocked at the coincidence of her having exactly what I needed. "How much for one?"

She put them back in the bag, keeping one in her pincer.

"Take it." She stuck it in my palm and curled her hand around it, making mine into a fist. "Maybe wearing the pin will give you some mojo to help solve the crimes like your Poppa would've."

I opened my mouth to protest, but quickly shut it when she tapped the bottom of my chin.

"It's not ladylike to gawk with your mouth open. If you let your mama mother you, I'm sure she'd have taught you that. I'll see you tonight." She turned away as if her jab was everyday talk and darted across the street, but not without flipping the bird to another car that almost hit her.

Chapter Nine

By the time I got home, it was dark. There was no sense in going to Kim's Buffett this late. It wasn't like I was going to get any more answers about Doc's murder tonight and any evidence wouldn't be back this quick.

I owned a little cottage off Broadway Street on the south side of Cottonwood, known as "Free Row." Everyone in town knew exactly where that was and not many people thought it was a good thing.

Most of the people who lived on my street were on commodity cheese and food stamps. Yeah, there were cars in the front yard propped up on cement blocks, ripped-up couches on porches, and maybe an unruly teenager or two—who didn't think I knew they were unruly—but I gave them the stare down if I saw them outside to put a little fear in them. No one on Free Row ever bothered me or they knew I'd be loading more than my washer and dryer.

Living on Free Row didn't bother me. My house wasn't much, but it was my Poppa's and he'd left it to me in his will. Duke and I enjoyed it and that was all that mattered.

"Hey, buddy." Duke had his paws and nose pressed up on the front window. When I opened the door, I saw the blinds had come crashing down on the hardwood. I bent down and gave him a good scratch while I let him lick my face. "You smell like Jolee's food truck."

I pulled back and looked at his nose. The edges were dotted with white powder. Duke was known to get into baking flour a time or two and I was sure today was no different.

I picked up the blinds and shook them toward him. "I guess another set of blinds bite the dust." I leaned them up against the wall.

Screwing them back up was going to have to wait. I was tired, I needed a bath, and I was hungry.

He tucked tail and darted off down the small hallway.

My house was small. It had two bedrooms on the far end of the house with a Jack and Jill bathroom between them. The family room and kitchen were down the small hall on the opposite side of the bedrooms. The family room was in the front of the house. Behind it, in the back of the house, was the kitchen.

A good cup of decaf coffee would be nice after a long hot shower, plus I needed to let Duke out into my fenced-in backyard. When it came to living on Free Row, Duke was even more effective than my gun. His size made people think twice.

"'Bout time you got home."

My skin crawled like someone had dragged their nails along a chalkboard. I knew who was in my kitchen before I even turned the corner.

Without looking at Mama, I went over to the coffee pot, grabbed the carafe and stuck it under the sink, turning the faucet on.

"If you were going to break and enter, the least you could've done is make a pot of coffee." I kept my eye on the rising level of water. "I didn't see your car out front. What are you doing here?"

"Your daddy had to go to the Jaycee's club meeting." Mama never did like to stay by herself when Daddy was gone.

The Jaycee's was really a club for men up to forty. Daddy was far past forty, but he was their main consultant, grand poo-pa in the community. Even though he complained that no other businessman in Cottonwood would step up to the plate, secretly I knew he loved it.

"We heard about Doc's murder and the jewelry store break-in. I figured I'd better stop by and hear about it for myself instead of gossip from the Euchre club." She drummed her fingers along the table. The drumming stopped, but the pointing began. "This *occupation* you have decided to go into."

"Mama, I won't have you coming into my house and telling me that I need to go to beauty school and work at Tiny Tina's." I slammed the faucet off and set the pot of water on the counter so I could let Duke out.

He had already scratched the hell out of the door casing; the last thing I needed him to do was tunnel a hole through the outside wall.

Mama stood up when I came back into the kitchen. "Look at you," she said. It was like I was looking into a mirror. "You look tired. You are a young woman. Vibrant and of the marrying age."

It was hard looking like her. All the men in town always told me how pretty she was and how lucky I was and that any man that stole my heart was going to be lucky too. She wore her hair long, like mine, and though her olive skin did have a few more wrinkles than mine, she was still gorgeous. She and I stood about the same height, five feet five inches, and we had the same body type, though she had a little wider hips. We had curves in the right places. We weren't too thin or heavy. And we wore the same size eight shoes.

Life between us was great once. She was my best friend, until I told her what I wanted to do with my life. That was the day it all changed.

"Oh, Mama." I threw my hands in the air. "Who on earth am I going to marry from Cottonwood?"

She shrugged. She knew I was right. There were no men in Cottonwood, not single anyways.

"And I'm sure Daddy is fine." I shook my head. "Otherwise, he'd have called me himself."

"Well, you are killing him." She sashayed over in her Capri khaki pants and yellow short-sleeved tennis shirt. She took the pot of water off the counter and poured it into the coffee maker. "And living on Free Row doesn't help either." She twirled her finger in the air. "One of these people in your own backyard is probably who killed Doctor Walton and broke into Viola's place."

"It was good enough for Poppa."

"It was different then." She was good at reminding me. "Do you have any leads on who killed Doc?"

I leaned my hip against the counter and crossed my arms. "You know I can't tell you anything about the investigation."

"I'm worried about you." She flipped the coffee maker on. "After all, you are the one responsible for putting yourself in this situation and my only child."

She wouldn't be my mama if she wasn't worried.

"And I'm going to be fine." I sucked in a deep breath. Fighting with her was not on my priority list. Her complaining wasn't going to change anything. "I'm getting a shower." I shook my head and headed down the hall to end the conversation.

It took a lot for me to not get into a screaming match with my mama. She'd start on her hissy fit and get me worked up before bed. I wasn't about to let her get the upper hand. Not in this case. This was real sheriff business.

I turned on the hot water as high as it would go and steam rolled out into the bathroom as I got undressed. The bathroom mirror quickly fogged. I took Poppa's pin off my sweatshirt and carefully laid it on the little glass shelf above the toilet. Sticking my hand under the water, I jerked it right back out and turned on the cold water, making it a desirable temperature and not one that would require me to go to the clinic for third-degree burns.

I stepped in and pulled the shower curtain closed, letting the water run over my head with my eyes closed. Images of the day kept popping inside my head though I tried to just enjoy the moment. The stick symbol bugged me, as did the stab wounds. The idea of mercury poisoning made my skin crawl. Who would think of something so awful? Wasn't the stabbing enough? This killer was vicious, and I had to get him or her behind bars before the community found out just how awful the murder truly was.

Finn. I made a mental note to give him a call to see if he'd found anything else at the jewelry store. Then there was Wyatt. I had mentioned to him that I was going to see if he could get appointed as my temporary deputy, but he never gave me a definitive answer. I thought I better call him before it got really late.

I jumped out of the shower and grabbed a towel. Without drying myself off, I darted back down the hall to grab my phone. It was getting late and I didn't want to wake up Wyatt if he was sleeping.

"The coffee smells good." Wearing only the towel, I stopped in the doorway of the kitchen. Then I saw Finn sitting at the kitchen table while Mama scurried around to get him a cup of coffee.

"Your friend Finn stopped by." Mama acted like she had the best southern manners in the world as she opened the cabinet to get a coffee mug. "Nice young man. Don't ya think?" Mama turned around.

Finn's mouth dropped. He threw his hand up over his eyes and tucked his chin to his chest.

"Kendrick Lowry!" Mama shrieked, dropping the mug, which shattered all over the kitchen tile floor. She rushed over, throwing her arms around my shoulders and pushing me back down the hallway into the bathroom. "This is why you need a good paying job. Stop pretending to play Nancy Drew all day long. When are you going to grow up?" She shoved me in the bathroom, slamming the door behind me.

I looked at the full-length mirror on the closed door at my reflection. It was still framed in steam from the hot shower, but the full image of me standing there dripping wet with a towel was right there. There I stood, with my long honey-colored hair plastered to my head, dripping big drops of water down onto my towel. Only the towel looked like moths had eaten it. There were holes in it exposing parts of my body that didn't need to be exposed, leaving Finn with an eyeful of things he shouldn't have seen.

"Get some new towels!" Mama screamed from behind the closed door, followed up by stomping feet and a slam to what I hoped was the front door.

A little giggle escaped me, turning into a hysterical laugh that caused me to take a seat on the edge of the tub, looking at myself in the full-length mirror. As much as I tried to keep it in, the laughter poured out of me and tears piled up on my eyelids. I had heard about these moments of insane laughter but had never experienced one until now.

I felt like I was on the edge of insanity and in an episode of *This Is Your Life*, because today had been eerily similar to both.

The image of Mama huffing it down Free Row's sidewalk made me cackle more. My stomach hurt as I doubled over trying to catch my breath. The knock at the bathroom door brought my laughter to a halt.

"Are you okay in there?" Finn's voice was borderline concerned, a "do I need to call the paddy wagon to come get you" concern.

I fanned my hand in front of my face, but not without a big smile.

"I'm happier than a dead pig in the sunshine," I called out, knowing I was going to have to face him at some point. After all, he was standing in my hallway trying to check on my mental status.

"Well..." Finn paused. "I'm not sure what that means, but I'm going to let you get some rest. I think you might need it."

"Of course you don't know what that means," I mumbled. The fit of laughter left my body as quickly as it came. Too bad. "When a pig dies while in the sun, the sun dries out the body and pulls its skin tight, leaving the pig with a toothy grin. Get it now?"

"Huh," Finn said flatly.

"I called Betty at dispatch to get the mayor to schedule an emergency town council meeting. I think I need to appoint Wyatt deputy until this is solved." I clamped my teeth together and squeezed my eyes shut when there was silence from the other side of the door as he hesitated. I didn't want to hurt his feelings like he wasn't helping, but he was only here temporarily. Who knew how long the reserves would let me keep him here. "I'm hoping to get a meeting set for tomorrow night."

"We can grab dinner beforehand if you want so I can tell you what I find out," he finally said.

"Did you find out anything yet?" I was curious as to why he had stopped by or even found out where I lived. It wasn't like he couldn't ask any Joe Schmo off the street. Everyone knew everyone and everyone's business. That's just the way it was in a small town.

"Nothing real solid," he said. "I'm still going down the list of patients we divided. I hope to have those done by tomorrow night."

"Great. Ben's before the meeting if Betty can get it set up by then?" I asked.

"Yeah. See you then," Finn said, followed by footsteps.

"Shut the door on the way out," I said so I could come out of hiding. I had to admit, I was a little embarrassed he saw me in my towel. A little more of me than I wanted him to see. But it was worth the look on my mama's face.

I didn't tell him to lock it. No one on Free Row ever bothered me, and I dared them to now—especially after the day I'd had so far.

Chapter Ten

The next morning while my coffee was brewing, I took Duke on a quick run. I wasn't sure if I was going to take him with me since I'd hopefully be chasing some leads on the two investigations. I didn't like the idea of keeping him in the car all day, so letting him get in a little exercise this morning to get out some energy was the plan, though it was a good stress relief for me too.

I poured myself a cup of coffee and sat down at the table. I dialed my parents' phone number.

"Good morning," Mama sang into the phone. She was always a morning person. "Lowry residence."

"Good morning, Mama." I took a sip of coffee to let her digest that it was me calling so early. "I wanted to make sure you made it home last night after you left here on foot."

"Why, Kenni." Mama gasped. "You waited this long to call? I could've been dead on the side of the road or kidnapped in one of your neighbors' creepy houses and you'd've never known."

"Mama, if someone kidnapped you, they'd give you back because you'd wear them out with all your talking," I assured her. "I just wanted to tell you good morning."

"Good morning." She sounded like a spoiled brat, which I blamed on Daddy. He always did spoil Mama and gave her everything she wanted. "Are you going to be looking for clues in the murder?"

"Goodbye, Mama." I sighed. "I'll call you later." I didn't offer her any other chance to talk before I hung up the phone.

I gave Duke some kibble and freshened up his water bowl

before I went to take a shower and get ready for the day. I feared it was going to be a long one. My first stop into town would be Kim's Buffet. She didn't open up until eleven for lunch. I'd take my time to get ready since I already knew I was going to be home late tonight.

When I turned off the shower, the phone was ringing. I let it go to the answering machine, but no one left a message. When the phone rang four more times and didn't leave any message, I knew someone was trying to get in touch with me.

This time I made sure I was dried off well, and retrieved another towel from underneath the cabinet that was in better shape than the last one. Granted, there were still a couple of holes, but not nearly as many as the drenched towel on the floor.

I gripped the edges of the towel around me while I grabbed the old yellow rotary phone hanging on my kitchen wall, then pulled the tangled-up cord apart while trying to let Duke in.

"Kenni, where are you?" Betty Murphy quipped from the other end. "I've been calling you on the dispatch walkie-talkie but you aren't answering me."

"I'm at home trying to take a shower before I put on my Wonder Woman cape for the day." I knew it was a smart-aleck thing to say and quickly regretted being mean. "I'm sorry, Betty. I'm a little on edge. What's up?"

"You aren't going to be any happier. Doolittle Bowman called and said to expect a big turnout at the town council meeting tonight. She even asked local area businesses to close."

Closing shop wasn't much of a big deal because most of Cottonwood closed down by nine p.m. anyway on a weekend, seven p.m. on weeknights.

"That doesn't make me unhappy." I wasn't sure why the news that really wasn't news would make her think I'd be upset.

"Can I finish?" Her sarcasm didn't go unnoticed. She continued, "She said everyone is in an uproar and they're demanding something be done." Betty talked so fast my ears couldn't keep up. All I understood was I was going to be hanging in the middle of Main Street from the big oak tree on the courthouse lawn if I didn't have some answers before the meeting.

"That's fine. I had expected as much. I'll have some information for the good people of Cottonwood," I lied into the receiver. It was better to go along with what the community wanted, and right now they wanted to be reassured that there was no need to be afraid. "I'm glad it's scheduled for tonight. Good work."

"You do have some information?" Betty asked, curiosity in her voice.

"Thanks, Betty." I hung up, not giving her any of the details I didn't have. I knew if I'd said a word, everyone in town would know before sundown.

Sunlight peeked through the front windows in the family room. Duke lay on the floor sunning himself in the stream. I walked over and bent down, running my hand along his warm body. Eagerly he groaned, rolling over on his back for a good belly rub.

With my towel securely wrapped around me, I lay in the stream of sunshine next to him and let the sun hit my face while I scratched his belly. Before I knew it, my eyelids got heavy, and closing them, I went off into a realm of unconsciousness.

Images of Doc Walton's Sharpie tattoo and the spray-painted carpet from White's danced in my head in some sort of weird pattern, along with images of Finn sweet-talking everyone who came into his line of vision, including Lulu and my mama. Oddly I found myself standing in the background, my Poppa standing behind me.

"You don't want to stay back here. You are a Sims. Not by name, but DNA. You take control of this situation," my Poppa's voice whispered in my ear.

"But I don't know what to do," my dream self pleaded with him. "I don't know how to look for clues in a murder. Please help me."

"You have this." Poppa's finger touched my chest right where my heart lay. A warm feeling, like the sun on my face, overtook the very breath in my lungs and every single beat of my heart. "And this." He held out the pin I had found in the truck and placed it in the palm of my dream self's hand.

"But I want you. I need you to guide me." There was a frantic feeling swirling inside almost like a panic attack; I desperately didn't want my Poppa to go back to where he had come from. I felt my real self coming out of my dream. "No!" my dream self screamed. "Don't send me back! Don't send me back alone!"

I jumped up when I felt Duke lick my cheek. My heart sank, as did my stomach, when I realized I was in the present in a towel with the sun beaming down on me.

"Hey, buddy."

I ran my hand over my forehead where sweat had beaded along the hairline and glanced up at the anniversary clock I had gotten from Ruby's Antiques when I first bought the place. The plate on the anniversary clock read "Congratulations to Dick and Bob." I didn't question where Ruby got it nor did she offer, though she did tell me it was from a breakup. Lucky for me that Dick and Bob didn't work out, because I got the perfectly used clock for a few bucks.

Regardless, the clock said I hadn't dozed off long and that I better get going if I was going to have anything to report to the town council tonight.

"You're right," I told myself in my bathroom mirror after I had gotten dressed in my sheriff's uniform. "I am a Sims and I'm going to prove them wrong."

"Damn right you are." The voice came from behind me. The same voice I'd heard whisper in my ear all day long yesterday.

I jumped, looking around. No one was there.

"Hello?" I cautiously walked into the kitchen, slowly grabbing for my holster. I unsnapped my gun and held it down to my side with my finger on the trigger. Slowly, I walked down the hall, swinging my gun in front of me and sticking my head in each of the bedrooms, finding them empty. I continued on my search. "Come on out. I know you're here."

Maybe I should rethink the whole not-locking-my-doors concept.

The entire house was empty but I swore I'd heard someone.

"I'm not crazy. I'm not crazy," I repeated, bringing my gun down to my side. I sucked in a few deep breaths to help calm the anxiety bubbling up inside of me.

I stood there for a few minutes and when I didn't hear anything else, I knew my subconscious had to be letting my parents and these crimes get to me. Mama and Daddy were begging for this day to come so I would quit the job and prove them right. Finn Vincent might have been called in a few days from now, but I was sure my father had used his pull with my Poppa's contacts to bring him in right from the beginning.

"I'm going to prove you wrong." I pointed to the framed picture of my parents my mother had given me as a Christmas present. "So I wouldn't forget where I had come from" were her exact words.

"Yes, you are," the voice confirmed. Only this time I saw a man, standing with his back to me.

"Hold it right there!" I screamed and pulled my arms straight up, pointing my gun directly at him. "I've got a gun and I'm not afraid to use it!"

My eyes darted around the room, making sure he didn't have a partner.

"Are you the killer?" I asked, lowering my voice so it wouldn't shake like my hands. "No, Duke." I called for Duke when he started to saunter over to the man.

Duke looked at me with his droopy eyes before he picked up his bone and kept walking.

Duke nudged the man's leg like he always did with my Poppa when he was a puppy. I had gotten Duke eight years ago from my Poppa as a high school graduation gift. It was six years later when Duke and I were home for a visit when I found Poppa dead.

"Not now, Duke," the man called out to my dog.

"How do you know my dog?" I asked through gritted teeth.

The voice was becoming clearer to my ear. It sounded a lot like my Poppa's. "Do you live around here?"

Something slid across the floor and stopped at my toe. I bent down and picked up my Poppa's pin that I was sure I'd left in the bathroom before my shower.

I rolled it between my finger and thumb, confirming it was real. My mouth went dry. My pulse throbbed in my fingers and my breath quickened. The air in the room was thick and stale. I gasped for breath.

"I've lost my mind." I shuddered inwardly at the thought of going to the psych ward in Lexington. I brought my arms back down to my side.

"Don't be alarmed, Kenni-bug." The man who sounded exactly like my dead Poppa referred to me by the nickname he'd affectionately given to me. "I'm only here to help."

"Don't you call me that!" I eased myself around to the right of the room.

He was standing there as sure as I was. I wasn't going nuts. I had an intruder. Someone playing a sick joke.

The man turned around.

"Poppa?"

My entire world went black.

Chapter Eleven

When I came to, I had a throbbing headache. If Doc Walton were alive, I would have immediately gone to him and had him check me for some sort of brain tumor.

"What was that?" I took a deep breath and patted my trusty sidekick, Duke. "Obviously the stress is getting to me."

Duke nudged me with his head. I sat there with my hand on his head, making sure I felt steady enough to get up. I didn't feel dizzy, just the same sick feeling of having to solve two crimes that were somehow linked. The stick symbol found on Doc's body and the jeweler's floor were all the proof I needed. My Poppa's pin was on the floor next to me. Without giving too much thought to how it got there, I grabbed it and my gun before I got up.

Duke licked my face. The kitchen phone rang. I tried to get my wits about me before I stood up.

"That was one crazy dream." I shrugged off what had just happened and glanced up at the clock.

It had to be stress, because the Dick and Bob clock reported a time lapse of thirty minutes. Plus, I had heard about these power naps and how you can have strange dreams.

"Hello?" I picked up the phone, leaning my shaking body up against the counter.

"Sheriff." It was Wyatt. "I wanted to update you on the statements I took from Sterling and Polly."

"How did it go?" I asked, rubbing my head. I stuck the phone between my ear and my shoulder and grabbed the ibuprofen off the kitchen windowsill. I dumped the coffee from my coffee cup into the sink and filled it up with tap water.

"Both of their stories panned out. Sterling had gone to get his hair cut and by the time he walked to Doc's, Doc had been dead a while." I listened and popped the two pills in my mouth and took a drink. "Viola White did have Polly work for her and according to Polly's mother—"

"Her mother?" I interrupted him.

"Her mama brought her down to the station," he said.

"But it was her dad that picked her up from White's." I didn't recall seeing her mother in his car, but I clearly wasn't thinking straight and could've been wrong.

"It was her mother, and according to her, Polly was at home and getting ready right up until it was time to drive into Cottonwood and open the shop." He wasn't telling me anything that I needed for the meeting.

"Well, the council meeting has been scheduled for tonight. You're going to be able to come, right?" I waited for a second and when he didn't answer I reminded him, "Remember I'm going to suggest they appoint you deputy until we can have a proper election."

"Can I do that and be jailer?" A good question, since we were both elected positions.

"I guess Doolittle will let us know tonight." That was the least of my worries. If Wyatt couldn't legally be sworn in as deputy, he'd still help out. Plus I had Finn, hopefully for as long as needed.

"If you get a minute, why don't you run on down to White's and see if you can find anything out of place?" Not that I didn't trust Finn, but Wyatt was part of the community and he'd know if something was out of place more than Finn. "Finn did a good sweep of the place, but I'd like it if you could too."

"I'm a step ahead of you."

It was great that Wyatt was being so helpful. It took a lot off my mind. My possibly crazy mind. "Finn was down there and I told him he could go since I had swept the scene and there wasn't much more to see. I kept the tape up so you could go and clear the scene."

"Sounds good." I really was appreciative of how Wyatt had stepped up to help out.

After we said our goodbyes, I walked into the kitchen, adjusting my holster around my waist, snug the way I liked it. I put the power nap, which sounded better than "blacking out," out of my mind. If it happened again, I would definitely make an appointment with Camille Shively. After all, she was the only doctor in Cottonwood now.

"You stay here," I ordered my sad-sack dog. It was clear that it wasn't going to be fair to Duke for him to sit in a car all day. His long droopy ears cocked back, flipping them inside out, and his already sagging eyes looked even slouchier.

"You are good at the pouty face, Duke. I'll have Jolee stop by. You love her." I patted his head, slid my hand over the counter, and grabbed my keys.

I forced myself not to look back because one too many times I had done the double take and given in to him. Today couldn't be one of those days. I had official business and didn't need a slobbery sidekick. Duke the hound dog had to stay home like every other dog in town.

An uneasy feeling settled in my stomach when I stepped out of the house and looked down the sidewalk on Free Row. The strange dream I'd had felt so real and as much as I tried to shake it off, I couldn't. It was like I could hear Poppa and almost touch him. Duke even played the part as he had done years ago. The dropping of the bone and nudging Poppa's leg was just as real in my dream state as it had been in real life. And I couldn't explain how the pin made it from the bathroom to the family room.

I took my phone out of my pocket and quickly dialed Jolee, leaving a message for her to let Duke out a couple of times on her travels for Meals on Wheels. Another thing On The Run food truck was good for. I'm sure she was slammed with between breakfast and lunch clients. I had no idea where she'd park the truck or I would've stopped by on my way to Kim's.

Within minutes I was in the old Wagoneer and turning left on Main Street to head down to Kim's Buffet. I wanted to show Mrs. Kim the picture of the symbol without giving too much away. I put the strange dream about Poppa in the back of my head.

I pulled the old Wagoneer into the empty parking spot right in front of White's, which was across the street from Kim's. The police tape Wyatt had strung up in front of the jewelry store had a big knot tied in the middle where Viola had snapped it. Sterling Stinnett stood in front of it wearing one of the five-point plastic sheriff pins I gave out to children.

He stood with his arms across his chest and legs apart, staring straight ahead.

I got out of the Jeep, grabbing my bag, and stood in front of him.

"Sterling?" I waved my hand in front of his stern face. "What are you doing?"

"Permission to move, Sheriff Lowry?" Sterling asked in a drill-sergeant voice. His hand rose to his brow as if he was saluting me.

"Um." I glanced to see if anyone was around. This town had gone nuts. Not that Sterling Stinnett wasn't a few fries short of a Happy Meal already, but this was even stranger than usual. "Yes."

"Shoo-wee." Sterling let out a long satisfied sigh. He tapped his finger on the plastic badge attached to his overalls. "I've been doing a good job as deputy in training."

"Deputy in training?" I asked.

Yes, this town had definitely gone crazy, me included.

"Wyatt gave me the temporary badge and said if I was able to stand here and not let anyone in, that I might be up for the sheriff's deputy job." Sterling's eyes sparkled and he couldn't stop grinning even when he tried to press his lips together. They quivered and reopened in a wide grin.

"He did, did he?" I asked. Wyatt didn't mention Sterling on the phone when I asked him about the jewelry store. "Did he say when he'd be back?" I wondered when Wyatt was going to release Sterling since I was really going to clear the place.

"Nope." He cleared his throat. "I mean," his head dipped, "no, ma'am...er...Sheriff." He stomped his foot on the ground. Like the wave you see at ballgames, the ripple started at his feet and stopped at his head when he straightened his body, like he was taking his post like a good soldier.

I guess he wasn't hurting anyone being there.

"Was there a guy about this tall, brown eyes, in a suit with him?" I asked. Wyatt said he'd told Finn he could leave, but I wondered if Sterling heard Finn mention where he was going. Finn was definitely the type of guy that would call me with any new developments.

"He left with Wyatt." Sterling didn't look at me; he kept his eyes straight ahead.

"No one's inside?" I asked, peering over his shoulder.

"Just Viola," he said. "Cleaning things up."

I pushed in the walkie-talkie button and turned my head toward my shoulder so Betty could hear me loud and clear. Wyatt had told me to go and clear the scene, but maybe Finn had done it.

"Betty?" I called for her, but didn't wait for her to answer. "Did anything come through about the theft at White's?"

"You mean did that hunk call in?" She let out a long sigh.

"Betty, this is official Cottonwood business over the dispatch." I reminded her to stay professional, even though she was right. "And yes. I'm referring to Finn Vincent."

As much as I didn't want to admit it, Finn Vincent was a hunk.

"Yes, Sheriff." Her stiff tone told me Betty's lip was stiff too. I had hurt her feelings and she was going to be all professional like she always did when I would correct her. "Officer Vincent called in. He said the evidence was collected and to call Mrs. White to let her know it was all clear. He found a calendar where she had cancelled an appointment with Art Baskin to set up a security system."

Art Baskin. I had completely forgotten about Art and his home security systems. He and Doc Walton were friends. I wondered if Doc had a home security system. Not that it would work if he had it off, but maybe there was a clue somewhere.

I put Art on the list of people to visit.

"Finn said that she should probably reschedule that meeting and get a system put in." Betty just talked and talked. I was getting good at drowning a lot of the nonsense out, but this caught my attention.

Why wouldn't Viola already have a security system in place? That seemed odd for a jewelry store, even in Cottonwood.

"Thank you, Betty."

I rolled down the volume button and turned back toward Sterling. Even though this was my investigation, I was glad Finn took the initiative to get the evidence sent off and Viola back into her shop.

I bit my lip. Maybe this town council meeting was a good time to voice my opinion on being short-staffed. Plus, Sterling wasn't doing anything to hurt the investigation since he was outside keeping guard.

"You are doing great. Do you mind ripping down all this police tape and throwing it away? Then you can go on about your day." I patted his arm and waited for a break in the light traffic before I darted across the street.

Kim's Buffett was busy with the lunch rush. Mrs. Kim was behind the counter taking orders from the long line of customers while Mr. Kim and their daughter, Gina, were behind them in the open kitchen slicing, dicing, and throwing soy sauce on everything in sight.

I moved my way around the crowd to the counter, not without feeling a few eyes on me.

"What you want?" Mrs. Kim's broken English had gotten better over the years. She always looked angry, but she squinted even more than usual now as she scowled at me. Gina had gone to great lengths to help her parents fit in in Cottonwood, but the Kims' attitudes still reminded me of drill sergeants. "We know nothing about the crime spree taking place here. Thinking of moving." Mrs. Kim's combativeness was apparent right away.

"I wanted to know if I could use your expertise for something."

The way I saw it, I could catch more flies with honey than vinegar, and being nice to Mrs. Kim was mighty important right now.

"Me? Expertise on the American law?" Her eyes opened a little more. Her lips pursed. "Hurry up." She flung her hands in the air. Behind her, Gina and Mr. Kim looked curiously over at me. "Don't you see I have a long line of customers here?"

"It will only take a second." I took the camera out of my bag and turned it on, flipping quickly through the images. I showed her the picture the thief had painted on the carpet at White's. "Do you know what this means?"

"Family." Mrs. Kim didn't hesitate, tucking a piece of her short black hair behind her ear. "Means family."

"Find out who the family is." The voice drifted through the air like a light breeze. I gulped.

"Are you alright?" Mrs. Kim asked without any emotion in her voice. "Kendrick? Your face all flush." Mrs. Kim never called me by my nickname. She believed in formality and a nickname was not up to her standards.

I closed my eyes, trying to get my wits about me. The voice was the same voice from my dream. My Poppa's. My face felt hot and my head began to spin. I held onto the counter with one hand, hoping the wave of crazy was going to pass.

"Gina, must hurry." Mrs. Kim's voice echoed in my head. "Hot tea," she ordered, her hand waving in the air.

"I'm fine." I opened my eyes and waved her off. I took another gulp. "Maybe a hot tea would be good." I sucked some air in through my nose and out my mouth.

"You need doctor. Stress too much for you." Mrs. Kim took the paper cup of tea and handed it to me. She pointed to the door. "You must go. I'm busy."

"Family." I held the camera back up to get one more confirmation.

"Yes." She didn't bother looking at me or saying goodbye; she simply pointed to the picture hanging on the wall with the same stick symbol in my photo. "Family. Next!"

Chapter Twelve

A picture of Camille Shively in a graduation cap and gown and all sorts of colored cord ribbons around her neck was prominently displayed in the waiting room of her office, surrounded by her endless diplomas.

The room was filled with several small brown leather loveseats and end tables, as well as inviting artwork, looking more like a living room than a waiting room. The trickling water fountain in the corner instantly calmed me, making me second-guess if I should've even stopped in without an appointment.

When I tried to sign in on the clipboard at the window, the receptionist immediately shooed me away and rushed to the back to tell Camille I was there.

"Kenni." Camille stood in the doorway leading back to her exam rooms with a smile. "Come on back."

"Oh, I can wait." I glanced around the room at the other patients who were staring at me like I had just cut in line.

"Don't be silly. Come on back," Camille encouraged me.

Her girl-next-door looks and good manners made it hard for anyone in Cottonwood not to find Camille endearing. Her hands were tucked in the pockets of her white coat. Her black hair was parted on the side and neatly hung past her collarbone. Her black eyes popped against her creamy white skin.

I fought my way out of the puffy cushions of the loveseat and found myself taking a seat in Camille's office.

"I'm going to finish up with a patient and I'll be right with you." She pointed to the coffee maker on the credenza behind her desk. "Grab a fresh cup," she said over her shoulder as she walked away, leaving me alone.

"Thanks." I took her up on her offer and poured myself a hot cup of coffee.

Being a doctor must be good. The can of Starbucks next to the coffee maker was a rare sight around Cottonwood. I was used to Ben's strong, stiff black cup of joe.

"I can't believe this." The familiar voice of Polly Parker came through the heating vent next to the credenza.

I put my steaming cup down and put my ear up to the metal slots of the vent.

"Is this forever?" Polly sobbed.

Camille was talking so low, I couldn't make out what she was saying, but I could make out Polly agreeing with her.

"I know it's not a death sentence." Polly sniffed, sucking in some mucus. "But this wasn't planned for my life. I mean, I want to be a mom. A wife." She sobbed again.

My eyes widened. What did she mean not a death sentence? She said she wanted to be a mom. What did that mean? Had I just become privy to some really good Cottonwood gossip I could never tell? No wonder Polly was so emotional at the jewelry store. She was hiding a big secret and it was up to me to find out what it was and if it had to do with Doc's death.

There were a few more hushed whispers coming from the vent and then a door shut. I jumped away from the wall and grabbed the cup of coffee.

"I hate what happened to Doctor Walton," Camille said as she walked back in the room. "And if you think I had anything to do with it because of the other day, I don't. I have proof of where I have been."

I kept a close eye on her body language. She fumbled with the file in her hand. The file folder and papers tumbled to the ground.

At the same time, we both bent down to pick them up, but I grabbed the most important information. The file was definitely Polly Parker's.

"Too much coffee." She brushed off her uneasiness. "Why are you here?" She shoved the papers back in the folder and stuck it on her desk.

I turned around and looked at her. She was prettier than a glob of butter on a mound of grits. That was a sight everyone in Cottonwood loved.

"I'm here about your confrontation with Doc Walton the day before yesterday at Ben's."

I was glad she brought up the subject first, though it made me awfully suspicious. It might even turn out to be small-town gossip, but I had to check out every clue.

"What?" A puzzled look crossed her face. "I just told you I have an alibi."

"Then you shouldn't mind my questions. It's all part of the job. Besides," I said as if it was no big deal, "I never said you had anything to do with his murder." Her fidgeting fingers caught my attention. "Why don't you tell me what the little heated discussion the two of you had was about?"

"Heated?" There was a certain undertone in her voice. She stuck her hands in the white lab coat. The blue stitching on the right side above her breast boasted her title, Dr. C. Shively. "Nothing. Forget I even said anything. Will I see you tomorrow night at Euchre?"

"Unfortunately, I can't forget that." I tapped my noggin. "Sorta why I got all this stress. I can't seem to forget anything dealing with Doc Walton." My brows lifted. "What happened?"

"Doctor-patient confidentiality keeps me from being able to say anything." She crossed her arms in front of her with a file tight to her torso, her body stiff. "We were discussing a patient we have in common. Had," she corrected herself.

"You can't give me any more? Not even a bitty bit?" I held my fingers up and parted them an inch apart, giving her another chance.

"Not even a bitty bit, Kenni." Her voice was flat.

"I can get a subpoena if that would be better." I loved throwing around the subpoena thing. For some reason that word made people vomit all sorts of information.

Poppa appeared behind her and bobbed his head back and forth trying to get a look at the file Camille was holding. My jaw dropped. I gasped for air.

"Are you sure that you're okay?" Camille put the file on her desk facedown.

"Dagnabbit." Poppa snapped his fingers in an "aw shucks" way and disappeared into thin air. I blinked a few times. Was I really seeing Poppa or was the stress getting to me?

"I'm just a little stressed about this whole thing. Plus, I hate to have to subpoena my friends." Calling Camille a friend was stretching it. Granted, we'd never mixed words, but we'd never gone shopping together either. Though there was Euchre.

Though it felt a little strange telling her, one of my peers, my issues, I wanted to talk about it. But it was hard to concentrate on me when I really wanted to see what was in that file and was wondering if my imagination Poppa could do ghost things like float in and between walls and windows. Who needed a warrant when I had Poppa? "With all the things," I emphasized the word things, meaning the murder and the break-in, "I think the stress is getting to me."

"Really?" She pushed a strand of her long black hair behind her ear, focusing her light black eyes on me. She seemed to relax as our conversation turned to my issues. "How so?"

"I know this is going to sound crazy, but I swear I keep hearing someone whisper to me." I could see she thought I was nuts. It was right there in her eyes. "I even had a dream about it." I left out the part about my ghost and how I thought it was Poppa.

When Poppa died, I wasn't sure if I was going to be able to carry on with my life. He meant that much to me. And the only way I'd felt a connection with him after his death was by becoming sheriff. Somehow it made me feel close to him.

"Kenni." Camille reached out and took my hands into hers. "Stress does funny things to our minds and bodies. It's only natural for you to react in such ways. And I'm writing you a prescription to get a massage down at Tiny Tina's." She let go of my hands and walked around her desk. She grabbed the fancy long silver pen out of a penholder with a tiny plaque boasting her credentials. The pen made a slight scribbling sound as she wrote something on a piece of paper. "You need to make sure during this investigation that you take time out for yourself."

"I don't think a massage is going to do it." I laughed, wondering who was really the crazy one, her or me.

"I'm serious, Kenni." She held her pointer finger and middle finger toward me, the piece of paper stuck between the two. "Stress plays with our minds and if you don't get a handle on it naturally, you won't be able to solve the murder or the theft." She walked around to the front of the desk and leaned her butt up against it. She looked down her nose at me. "You are up for re-election in a couple of years. You and I both know that the way you conduct this investigation and how it's solved could be your legacy."

She was right. Small-town politics could get ugly, and if I wanted to be re-elected, now was not the time to act nuts.

Reluctantly, I took the paper from her and opened it. She had written: "Take care of yourself. Get an aromatherapy massage."

"And if this doesn't work," she walked over to the door and opened it, my cue to leave, "then we will look at alternative means. Got it?"

"Yes." I stood up and walked out into the hallway. "But Tiny Tina's idea of a spa is a vanilla extract rub down. And a pedicure." I shook my head and rolled my eyes. "Don't get me started on how she thinks olive oil over a few of the rocks she dug out of the town branch was worth thirty dollars. Though this will make my mama happy if she hears I stepped inside of Tiny Tina's."

That was no joke. Someone would see me go inside the shop and call Mama immediately. Mama would nearly break her arm patting her own self on the back thinking she talked me into going to beauty school after all.

"Kenni, it was great seeing you."

Camille pushed me out into the waiting room.

"If you do decide to cooperate without a subpoena, you know where to find me." I had to throw in one last try. "Because I will get the warrant."

"I'll be looking for it." Camille smiled sweetly and shut the door.

There was really nothing I could do right now if she didn't want to tell me her little secret. It might take some time to get a warrant. But it wasn't like I couldn't get one, and Ronald Walton wasn't going anywhere.

Camille Shively just went on my short list of suspects.

Chapter Thirteen

"I don't know what is going on with me, but Tiny Tina's is not going to do it." I sighed, driving down South Main and heading out of town back toward Bone Creek Road.

"That's right. Tiny Tina's, huh." Poppa harrumphed next to me on the passenger side. "There ain't nothing wrong with you."

The tires skidded when I veered off the road, bringing the Wagoneer to an abrupt stop.

Tears filled my eyes. I wasn't sure if it was because I was scared, I was going crazy, or how much I wished he were really there. "Listen, mister. I'm not sure who you are or if you are even real or if I've gone crazy." I took a deep breath. An unrecognizable laugh escaped my body. I beat the steering wheel with the palm of my hand. "I'm crazy!" I screamed while flailing my arms about. "I'll be damned. Mama and Daddy were right. This job has made me crazy."

I took a deep breath and grabbed the wheel. I squeezed my eyes shut, knowing that when I opened them and turned around, imaginary Poppa was going to be gone.

I opened my eyes. "Oh no." My plan had failed. I felt crazy. "You are not here. You are not here," I repeated and shook the wheel as hard as I could without it coming off the column.

"I know it goes against everything you have ever known about the afterlife." Poppa rested his elbow on the passenger door and drummed his fingers. "But I'm here. I'm real and you are the only one besides Duke who can see me."

"No, no, no," I repeated. Seething, I turned toward him. "You are not here and I'm not crazy."

"I am here and you are not crazy, Kenni-bug." He scooted a little closer. "You are the one who asked me to come help you."

"I did no such thing," I denied his words.

"Yes, you did. At my grave." He reminded me about my little visit to the cemetery. "And I'm here to help you with your first murder investigation." He ran his thick fingers over the three strands of brown hair he combed over to the side. "I tried. I did."

"Tried what?" I asked, deciding to give into the idea I was crazy and seeing things.

"It's been hell scaring off every single thief or criminal around here for the past two years." He sucked in a deep breath and held it for a few seconds like he always did before he released a long steady stream of air.

All the times Betty Murphy had called break-ins over dispatch only to find out they were false calls rolled around in my head.

"You have got to stop holding your breath." The words escaped my mouth just like they used to when he was alive and did this. "Scaring off criminals?"

"Yes. Since you were elected sheriff." He rubbed his hands together. "How do you explain a zero crime rate in Cottonwood since you took over?"

"I have Wyatt now." I decided to play with my crazy imagination. "So you can go back to the great beyond and give me my sanity back."

"I'm afraid I can't do that." Poppa stopped rubbing his hands together and planted them on his thighs. "I'm here to help you, Kenni-bug. Besides, Wyatt is the jailer."

"I don't need your help." I stuck my hand out to touch my imaginary Poppa.

"You can't touch me. I'm a ghost."

"A ghost?" I busted out laughing. My imagination had never been this good before. "I thought I might be going crazy. But now I *know* I'm crazy." I picked up the prescription from Camille and laughed. "I need Tiny Tina's more than I realized." I took out my phone and began to type in the number.

The phone flew from my fingertips and landed in the floorboard.

"You are not crazy." Poppa's chin lifted; his eyes held an icy gaze. The gaze he had when he meant business. I'd seen this look so many times when he went to court to make sure the criminals stayed behind bars. I spent many days in my youth going to the courthouse, watching Poppa do his job. I was fascinated.

"I forgot all about that face." I pointed and smiled at the fond memory, letting my guard down. "How exactly are you going to help me? Are you going to tell me who killed Doc Walton? That would help me."

If my mind was going to play games on me, I was going to ask my brain hard questions. I was not convinced imaginary Poppa was a ghost. A real ghost.

"I wasn't there," Poppa said.

"So you're telling me the one time there was truly a crime, Ghost Poppa decided not to show up?" I was beating my imagination.

"Something like that." Poppa was vague. "I can tell you about when Betty Murphy called you about a movie stolen from Luke Jones's theatre."

"But it wasn't." I vividly remembered going over to Luke's to make the report, but he'd found it somewhere in his closet. Though he said he didn't put it there, he obviously had. "It was in the closet."

"I put it there, because Polly Parker was the one who stole it."

"Polly Parker?" I questioned.

Poppa nodded his head.

"Fine." I picked up my pen and wrote Polly's name on my list of people to go see. "I need to see her about the jewelry break-in, so I'll ask her about it."

"Okay." Poppa crossed his arms. "And also ask her about Chance."

"Mayor Ryland?" I questioned. "Everyone in town knows it's just a rumor." My imagination wasn't going to fool me.

"Ask her about the cabin out on Chagrin Road." Poppa continued to spit out facts about things I had no clue about.

There was nothing on Chagrin Road but acres and acres of farmland.

"Fine." I turned the key of the ignition and started the car. I pulled back on to Bone Creek Road and headed straight toward Chagrin Road. It was now or never; time to put this imaginary ghost behind me so I could solve these crimes and get on with my life. "I don't need to ask her. I can drive there and see for myself."

Poppa didn't protest when I swerved the car around and headed out of town. He smiled. He was as happy as a newborn in a topless bar.

Chapter Fourteen

Poppa looked out the window. "Everything looks the same."

"It's not." I swung the wheel right on Holiday Road and grabbed the police light. "Nothing is the same." I was referring to myself. "I'm going to free my brain once and for all," I grumbled under my breath and rolled down the window. "I'm going to prove to you that there is not a cabin this side of Chagrin Road."

I licked the suction cup and slapped the light on top of the Wagoneer, flipping the switch on. I was on a mission to prove this ghost wrong.

"You know it's illegal to pretend there is an emergency," Poppa quipped from the back. I jerked around because I could've sworn he was just in the front seat next to me. He was always a stickler for rules and so was I...until now.

"My sanity is an emergency." I pressed the gas pedal as far down as it would go, knowing my engine would have its own little heart attack, but the sound helped drown out the loud unwarranted sighs of imaginary Poppa.

I turned on the gravel road. Chagrin Road.

"And you are here to check out my story about Ryland and Polly Parker, aren't you?"

"You are in my head, making me feel crazy, and I cannot carry on with a murder investigation without knowing what's real and what isn't." I was talking to him like he was really there. I pinched my leg. "Ouch," I gasped, rubbing my hand over my thigh to get the sting out. "I'm not going crazy. I'm not going crazy."

"There! Turn there!" Poppa pointed out the passenger window when I nearly missed the road.

I slowed the Wagoneer down and looked between the two trees imaginary Poppa was pointing to. The weeds were overgrown, taller than my tire wheelbase.

"I'll be damned." My stomach dropped when I saw tire tracks. My mouth open, my eyes slid back to smiling imaginary Poppa.

His cheeks balled from the big grin planted across his lips. "I told you. I'm here to help you, Kenni-bug."

I gulped. Was the ghost of my Poppa really here? I'd never believed in ghosts. Was he really the reason crime hadn't happened around Cottonwood since I was elected? Had he been looking out for me since?

Everything he had said about Luke Jones was right.

"See." Poppa pointed from behind the big oak tree we were hiding behind. I'd parked the car and got out so we wouldn't make noise going through the wooded land. I followed the batted-down weeds from the tire tracks until we got close enough. "Right through there is the mayor's love nest."

Fifty yards in front of us, nestled behind a few trees, was a small log cabin. The mayor's car and Polly Parker's were pulled up next to each other.

The gravel drive would definitely make noise if I ran up alongside the house to get a good look inside, so I slipped my shoes off and tried the best I could to tiptoe up to the small cabin.

"Ouch. Ew. Ouch." I couldn't help but let out the pain from the edges of the rocks sticking the bottom of my foot.

"Shh." Poppa was already up to the side of the house, looking in the window. "They won't hear me, but they will hear you." He pressed his head clear through the window, the rest of his body still on the outside of the cabin. "They're fussing."

"About what?" I asked in a hushed whisper, a safe distance from the house. I squatted by Polly's front tires. If Poppa was going to tell me everything they were saying, I didn't need to risk being seen.

"He's telling her it's not the end of the world." Poppa drew back, looked at me, and shrugged. He stuck his head back through the window. "Crap! Here they come!"

"What?"

It didn't take long to know he was right. The cabin door creaked opened and Polly walked out, stopping on the porch. Her face was red and blotchy. It was shameful, but I took a little pride in the fact that she had an ugly cry face.

Polly and Mayor Ryland stood on the porch. He said a few words I couldn't hear because I was too busy slipping underneath Polly's car. I rolled completely in the middle so if she drove forward or backward, she wouldn't run over me. I became one with the gravel, or so my body felt like it.

The sound of my heart and footsteps surrounded me. I took one deep breath and held it, waiting for Polly to get in the car.

"Let's go back in and talk about it, baby," Mayor Ryland pleaded with Polly. The toes of their shoes were touching.

"But you won't love me. This was not in our plan," Polly pouted.

"Baby, this can be worked out," he assured her. The toes parted and the sound of footsteps faded back into the cabin.

"See, I can help you solve these crimes." Poppa was crouched down by the car, his head tipped under the bumper looking at me.

"You can't go around scaring me like that," I warned, my hand on my heart. I rolled out from under the car and ran as fast as I could back to the Wagoneer. The stabs on the bottom of my feet didn't faze me. I had to get out of there.

"Come on," I yelled when I realized Poppa wasn't with me. It kinda felt silly yelling for a ghost, but deep down I was happy he was here. With my keys in hand, I jumped in the Wagoneer. Poppa wasn't in the car and for a second, I waited.

"What am I doing?" I jabbed the keys into the ignition and looked for Poppa before I slammed the pedal down. "He's a ghost. He can catch up." I glanced in the rearview mirror, making sure I was way out of sight of Mayor Ryland and Polly Parker.

Chapter Fifteen

"Where are we off to now?" Poppa sat in the front seat as proud as a peach. There was fire in his eyes. There was no denying how much he enjoyed the chase of a criminal.

Whether or not my mind was playing havoc with me, it tickled me to no end to see my Poppa's feistiness that I had long buried in the back of my mind since his death.

"Are you going to go ask Polly Parker about the movie she stole from Luke?" Poppa asked. "Then you really might believe I'm who I say I am and that I'm here to help you."

"No. I'm going to the office." I kept my hands on the wheel, trying not to fight my internal struggle. I couldn't decide whether I was going crazy or if Poppa was really here to help me.

It was like one of those ghost shows on TV. They made it believable on *Ghost Hunters*, but now that it was happening to me in real life, it was a different story. One thing I knew for sure, there were crimes that needed to be solved, and the evidence taken from the crime scene that I had Wyatt send off to the lab should be back soon.

"So if you're here to help me, let's go through this." I went ahead and decided to give it a try. "Camille Shively would seem like a likely suspect because they had a disagreement in public, though I don't know what that was." I held up my finger. "Yet."

"I'm sure if you keep threatening to get a warrant, she might cave." Poppa had easily gone back into his sheriff mode. "Then there's the 'family' symbol on Ronald and at White's. That has to mean something. And don't forget about Viola White." Poppa was so good at making checklists of suspects when he was sheriff.

"And why didn't she have a security system?" I really did find that odd. "With all that money and jewels in the case."

"What would her reason be for killing Ronald?" Poppa had that look. Curiosity. "Kenni-bug, things aren't adding up."

"I really don't think Polly or Mayor Ryland are related to the crimes, but it does make juicy gossip." I giggled and turned into the alley behind Cowboy's Catfish. I parked the Wagoneer behind the dumpster in my normal parking spot.

"That is something you don't need to get caught up in," Poppa grunted.

"Then you shouldn't have told me," I grunted and turned off the ignition.

"I told you so you would believe I was here." He had a point.

"Good afternoon, Betty." I shut the door behind me with the heel of my boot.

"Late afternoon." Betty glanced up at the clock above the only jail cell we had in Cottonwood.

Having a jail cell and office located in the back of Cowboy's Catfish was not an ideal spot, but we were just a small town. If we ever really did need to hold someone who was a real threat to the community, we would transport them to a bigger city. Until then, there was no need to build a real jail.

The space was plenty big for Wyatt, Betty, and me. There were three desks. One for me, one for Betty, and the other for Wyatt. There was a cement-block room next to our office where we put a cot, blanket, and pillow. The only time the room was used was when Wyatt brought someone in to sober up. Most of the time, he'd drive them home.

"Betty sure hasn't aged." Poppa stood so close to Betty, I swear I thought she could see him. She shivered up one side and down the next. She grabbed her cardigan sweater off the back of her chair.

"Did you feel that sudden chill?" she asked, fumbling with the buttons.

I shook my head. "Can you call Art Baskin and Wyatt? Tell them both to meet me at Doc's place first thing in the morning. Say around eight?"

"Is Art a suspect?" Betty's brow cocked.

"Don't go and spread any gossip." I thumbed through a file Wyatt had left on my desk. It was a fax confirmation from some paperwork he had sent to the lab. "Have you heard back from the lab yet? Fax or call?"

"No." Betty was hunched over her rolodex, twirling it with one hand while the other flipped the alphabet tabs.

"I'm telling you, if you use the computer life would be so much easier for you." I had spent the better part of the past two years trying to bring the office up to technology speed. Only I was afraid I'd have to get rid of Betty for that.

"Not going to happen. Not in my lifetime." She plucked the card out of the file and tapped away on the phone. "Art said he'll be there," Betty said after talking on the phone for a few minutes.

"What are you doing?" I asked Poppa. He had his nose stuck deep in the wireless modem I'd had Art install when I took office.

"I'm going home." Betty's purse was dangling from the crook of her elbow. "Unless you can think of anything else I need to do."

"No." I gulped, realizing I was talking out loud to Poppa in front of Betty. "I'm good."

"I almost forgot." Betty stopped shy of the door. She pointed to my desk. "That package on your desk is from Finn. Something about ear pieces."

"Thanks." I walked over and picked up the box. "Have a good night."

The county paid Clay's Ferry to take any Cottonwood dispatch calls during the off-hours. They'd call me directly if someone called, which was rare.

"I'll see you at the meeting, unless you want me to get you some supper at Cowboy's." Betty looked at me. I shook my head.

"I'm meeting Finn—um," I corrected myself, "Officer Vincent for supper at Ben's to go over a few things."

"Are you?" Her lips turned up in a grin. She didn't wait for me to answer. She gave a two-finger toodle-loo over her shoulder before she disappeared into Cowboy's Catfish.

Chapter Sixteen

I tucked the box from Finn under my arm and walked down Main Street to Ben's. There was no sense in driving since it was down the street, and the fresh air might do me some good. It wasn't like my morning jogs, but it still helped clear my mind.

"What is the star of the hour doing here?" Ben Harrison said when I walked in.

I wasn't sure if it was a greeting, but he had a big grin on his face. His brown shaggy hair was tucked up under his backward baseball cap, showing off his brown eyes. Ben was a looker. He was probably the cutest man in Cottonwood. And the fact that he cooked made him even more appealing.

"Don't you mean falling star?" I teased back, and pointed to Finn, who had taken the two-top table nestled in the corner.

"Fancy pants." Ben had on his normal attire of a plaid shirt, jeans, and a dishtowel flung over his left shoulder. "Who is he?"

"Finn, from Chicago, part of the Kentucky Reserves." Looking over at him my jaw tensed, and I tried to take a couple deep breaths without Ben noticing.

"Finn? Who has a name like Finn?" Ben looked over at Finn.

"Poets." I laughed. "He's a nice guy though. He's doing all he can to help out."

"Stressed out? Or attracted to him?" Ben's smile grew even bigger and brighter, showing off the great dental work of Beverly Houston. "I don't think I've ever seen someone get to you like this. Tough Kenni Lowry is frazzled by Finn."

"Neither. You are silly." I ran my hand over my hair. Finn was all sorts of handsome. Could Ben really see I was a little nervous having supper with Finn? Or that I did think he was somewhat attractive? I mean, it wasn't like it was a date. It was work. Just like me meeting Wyatt, only Wyatt was far from young and buff with a full head of hair like Finn. Not that I'd noticed.

"I'll put on a fresh pot." Ben turned and headed back to the counter. He knew exactly what I needed. "It looks like you're going to need it."

The night was going to be long and my mind needed to be on high alert. I had to be wide awake for the meeting.

"I was beginning to think you stood me up." Finn didn't look up from the plastic menu.

"You don't need to look at that." I plucked it out of his hands. "Everyone at Ben's gets the special. In fact," I stuck the menu between the salt and pepper shakers where it rightfully belonged as a decoration, "I don't think he even cooks half the stuff on the menu."

"Whatever you say, Sheriff." Finn grinned those fancy pearly whites.

"Look at you." I sat down, giving him a onceover. He had on a pair of dark jeans, a red plaid shirt, cowboy boots, and the biggest belt buckle you ever saw this side of the Mississippi.

His fancy suit was long gone.

"I didn't plan on still being here tonight. I went to the Tractor Supply store and this was the best they had." He looked different. A good different.

"Do you have any new leads?" I asked, moving my hands back when Ben walked over with two cups of coffee in his hands, setting them in front of me.

"No thanks." Finn waved off the large cup. "I'll have water."

"Oh, they aren't for you," Ben quickly corrected Finn. "Kenni always gets two cups."

Happily, I pulled them both in front of me and stuck my nose in the steam climbing up in the air, taking a deep inhale of the strongest black coffee in town.

"Two specials." I held up two fingers before wrapping my hand around one of the cups, bringing it up to my lips. "Tiny Tina doesn't have anything on you."

"Tiny Tina?" Ben's head cocked to the side.

"Nothing. Two specials," I repeated, keeping Dr. Shively's prescription to myself.

Neither he nor Finn needed to know about me telling Camille I was stressed. Ben would definitely not let me live it down.

Ben hesitated, but walked away.

"I went down the list of patients Doc Walton had on file and half of them couldn't hold a knife or arm-wrestle an infant, much less take down a man." Finn's perfectly manscaped brows cocked. "So I went back to the scene of the crime, and then I went to see Max."

"Max?" I asked, knowing Max probably told him about the symbol.

"He informed me that you stopped by and he showed me the symbol on Doctor Walton's wrist which I knew matched the symbol at the jewelry store." He tapped his finger on the table.

"I did find out from Mrs. Kim that the symbol means family. I've not figured out what that means to the crime, but we will." I nodded.

"I found these at the scene of the crime." He took his fancy phone out of his pocket and showed me a picture of some mud.

I squinted, tilting my head side to side trying to figure out what the picture was and trying not to look stupid.

"Tire tracks." He used his fingers to swipe the picture, making it bigger, something my little flip phone didn't do. He tapped the photo, causing it to go back to the original size. "So I'm guessing the killer got to Doc Walton's house by car. Old car, because the tires are small. Thin. And they were in the back of the house."

"Why do you think the killer parked in the back?" I wasn't following, so I decided to take another sip of coffee. Maybe it would jumpstart my brain. He sucked in a deep breath and stopped talking when Ben came back over with Finn's water.

Ben looked between us and smiled. I gave him the stink eye until he moved on.

Finn started again, "I noticed there were some smudge marks of dried mud by the back door. Smudged, as in deliberately trying to get rid of shoe prints. Shoe prints that shouldn't have been there if Doc didn't let anyone in his house with shoes on." Using his finger, he swiped through the photos again, showing me Doc Walton's kitchen floor, where there was definitely some muddy smudging going on.

"Finn, that's brilliant." I had forgotten about Toots telling us Doc didn't let anyone wear shoes. "The killer probably came in the back door and took Doc off-guard."

"The killer was also smart enough to drag the footsteps making trudge marks to the car. Whoever killed Doc Walton knew him and knew he didn't let people wear shoes inside." He showed me another picture. "But..." An evil grin crossed his face, his eyes boring into me with a twinkle set deep in them. "The killer wasn't smart enough to drag the tire tracks."

"Really?" I grabbed his phone out of his hands and looked at all the photos again.

Damn. He was good.

"I'm not a tire expert, so I need to know who is in Cottonwood, or I can send the pictures to someone from my division of the State Police." He made a good suggestion.

"Can you email those to me?" I asked. "I have someone who will know exactly what kind of car those tire marks belong to, but in the meantime, definitely send them out. We can use all the expertise we can get."

A couple minutes later and an email full of pictures sent to me, Finn and I were enjoying Ben's special.

"Ear pieces?" I patted on the box.

"Yeah. We had some extra at the Reserve office so I had them couriered down here." He took them out of the box. "It's much less bulky than those big walkie-talkies. And even better, not everyone can hear what you and Betty are talking about."

He handed me one over the table. He was right. These would definitely be better than the walkie-talkie, only I wasn't so sure I was going to like them in my ear.

"I'll give it a try if you get them set up for me." I wasn't willing to admit that the use of technology wasn't a strong quality I had.

He nodded and shoved a forkful of food in his mouth.

"Son of Sam," Finn mumbled through the mouthful of food out of nowhere.

"I don't know Sam." I racked my brain between chews trying to recall someone who lived in Cottonwood named Sam.

I was sure there had to be someone with the name Sam, but no one that I knew.

Finn swallowed and took a drink of water to clear his mouth.

"The movie, *Summer of Sam*." He set the glass down. "Don't tell me you haven't seen it."

"Okay, I won't tell you." I shrugged.

"You really haven't seen it?" he asked, as if my life depended on it.

"No. I haven't." I picked up my cup of coffee and held it up to my nose, taking a nice long inhale.

"I've been going over and over in my mind those symbols on Doc's wrist and the carpet of the jewelry store. It's a lot like *Summer of Sam*, which is about a terrible crime spree of a serial killer, Son of Sam. I'll leave out the gory details, but he left a note, a sign, behind on every crime, taunting the police." He took another bite. Through muffled lips, he said, "This reminds me of a pretty immature Son of Sam job. The symbol, as if the killer is taunting us. Trying to tell us something. The killer wants us to know the two are connected."

"A puzzle?" I asked, thinking that I had to rent *Summer of Sam*. Poppa appeared next to Finn. His nose almost touched Finn's cheek and his eyes were lowered. He was really getting a good look. He turned toward me. I kept eating, trying to ignore him since Finn was right there.

"I'm sure you've already realized that Luke could name the

exact tire from the marks. And if this whipper-snapper is right about *Summer of Sam*, you can ask Luke about it too. I bet he'd have a copy of the movie." Poppa discussed the evidence with me like he did when he was living. Even when I came home for a weekend visit from college, he loved to go over his cases with me. It became a sort of game between us. Only back then everyone could see him, not just me.

"I also saw what looked to be a video camera on the side of the barn behind Doc's house." Finn looked up over top his plate. He was definitely enjoying Ben's food. "Did he have a security system?"

"Funny you should ask." I had to admit, Finn was very observant. "I'm meeting with Art Baskin in the morning at Doc's to discuss that very thing."

"Art Baskin? Who is that?" Finn asked.

"Sorry, I keep forgetting you aren't from around here." I smiled. "He owns the only security system in Cottonwood and would be the likely company anyone around here would use. I want to ask him about White's and why Viola never used a security system."

Chapter Seventeen

"Alright! Alright!" Mayor Ryland stood behind the podium in the basement of Luke Jones's house, beating the wooden gavel and calling the emergency meeting to order. "Let's get this meeting started."

I looked around. Everyone was there. Rowdy, Wyatt, Camille, Ben, Viola, and Ruby were just a few of those standing in the back. The Kims sat in the second row, Mrs. Kim staring straight ahead.

"What is this?" Finn leaned over and whispered in my ear. He craned his neck in all directions, looking around.

I made sure we got a seat in one of the folding metal chairs in the front row so Finn could get an up-close look at how things in Cottonwood worked. He was fitting right in with the outfit and everyone came by to greet him before Mayor Ryland banged the gavel.

"Luke is gracious enough to let us use his basement, a.k.a. movie theatre, for town meetings." I pointed to the pull-down screen for the movies. "On good days, the screen is used. When the screen gets jammed and won't pull down Luke uses an old sheet."

On the wall was a movie poster of *To Catch a Thief*, the featured film for next week's showing, something I was definitely going to put on my calendar because I could probably use a tip or two. I wasn't sure what this week's movie was.

"Thank you for coming. Now we all know about the crime spree that is spreading like wildfire through our humble town." The mayor spoke very loudly. A collective groan filtered through the room. His eyes found me and they narrowed.

A sudden sob blurted out from the third row. I turned back to see who it was. Polly Parker. Her pretty little blonde head was buried deep against her father's chest. Inwardly I groaned, silently telling her to grow up. I couldn't help myself. I looked to see if her belly had a bump. She looked the same as she always had. I'd be sure to do a little more digging. "I'm going to turn it over to our sheriff, Kenni Lowry."

A lackluster round of applause didn't make me feel good.

"I called this meeting because we are a tight-knit community. I love our town and I think you need to know about its security." I looked out into the crowd. "I feel it is my duty to keep you informed."

All eyes stared at me. My palms began to sweat and palpitations started. I was clearly not ready to be a public speaker. Especially one whose audience had fear on their faces.

"First off, the festival is still on as planned." The crowd erupted in applause.

Edna Easterly wasn't hard to spot. The feathered fedora choice for tonight's emergency meeting was a lime green number. The feather was twice as long as the one she had worn yesterday, sticking out a foot taller than any head in the crowd. The darn thing waved in the air as her head bobbled back and forth trying to get her handheld tape recorder as close to me as possible. I was happy I was able to deliver good news. It was nice to see all the smiling faces after a few long, sad days.

"Take your time. Shine, Kenni-bug." Poppa gave me a double thumbs up and a toothy grin. I lifted my hand and touched his pin. I had accepted the fact that Poppa was here to comfort me through this stressful time.

"I have several leads in both cases, and since I cannot be in two places at once, Officer Finn Vincent has been sent by the Kentucky State Reserves to assist." I gestured for Finn to stand and wave to the group.

Heads bobbed and people propped up a little more in their chairs to get a look at the handsome man in the front row. A few mothers nudged their single daughters, nodding grins toward him.

"If you see him in town or he stops by to ask you any questions, it's okay to talk to him." Then I pointed to the right side of the room where Wyatt was leaning against the *To Catch a Thief* poster. "I also want to see if the council will take a quick vote to let Wyatt Granger become deputy sheriff since Lonnie Lemar has retired."

Wyatt's shoulder pushed off the wall and he stood up straight with his hands crossed in front of him. My eyes slid over to the front row where Finn was sitting.

Doolittle Bowman was busying herself flipping through some papers.

"This way," I sucked in another breath and got a little louder, "Wyatt can work on the recent," I made sure to stress the recent part, "crimes instead of hanging out in the back of Cowboy's Catfish."

"What's wrong with Cowboy's Catfish?" Bartleby Fry, owner of Cowboy's Catfish, chimed in.

"Nothing, Bartleby. I'm just saying that—"

"I've got this, Sheriff." Wyatt galloped onto the stage in front of the podium, and, caught off-guard, I lost my footing.

"Whoa." My arms twirled around like a whirly bird as I tried to balance on one leg before I tumbled off the stage, right into Finn's lap.

"Are you okay?" Finn asked, his face way too close to mine.

"Yeah." I gulped and looked into his big brown eyes.

A head crept over Finn's shoulder, blocking any and all light from the track lighting Luke had designed for his movie nights.

"Kenni-bug." The head slowly swayed back and forth. "I'll be. I see it in your eyes. You got a hankerin' for this boy."

My eyes closed. I opened them. Poppa was standing over Finn's shoulder. He had the biggest grin on his face. The warmth radiated from Finn's arms as they cradled me.

"Sheriff?" Finn asked. "Kenni?" The way he said my name was music to my ears. "Is there a doctor in here? I think..."

"I'm a doctor!" Camille Shively's voice came shrieking from behind.

Poppa made a kissy face.

"Poppa." The word came out of my mouth, making me sound like a six-year-old. I giggled and then realized what I had said. I threw my hand over my mouth.

"Poppa?" Finn's face contorted. The shadowy head moved and Luke's track lighting briefly filtered over Finn's shoulder right into my eyes until Camille's round face peeped over.

"Kenni Lowry, are you okay?" She held a small flashlight, darting it between my eyes.

"God," I held my hand up in front of my face, "I'll be blind if you don't stop shining that thing in my face. I'm fine. Just lost my footing, that's all."

I pushed her hand aside and myself up and out of Finn's arms, though they were strong and for some odd reason I felt really safe in them.

"Now that Sheriff Lowry is back on her feet..." Mayor Ryland stood next to Wyatt on the stage and cocked a brow toward me. He let out a long heavy sigh. "I want to bring us all to a vote. Those in favor of Wyatt Granger becoming Deputy Sheriff, raise your hand."

"Wait! Wait!" I waved my arms over my head and stepped right back up to the podium. I glared at Wyatt, who didn't seem to apologize for nearly killing me by knocking me off the stage. "This is a temporary position," I reminded them.

"Yes, temporary," Wyatt repeated.

"All in favor?" Mayor Ryland lifted both of his hands.

"Stop!" Doolittle Bowman tugged on the edges of her short brown hair and pushed her glasses up on her long nose. She held one of the pieces of paper she was shuffling up in front of her face. "The jailer can't hold any more than one elected position."

A low rumble of mumbling came from the crowd.

"Ya know, if Wyatt can't be appointed deputy because he is jailer," I heard Poppa's voice above the hushed whispers of the crowd, "you seem kinda fond of that young whipper-snapper.

Maybe he should be appointed temporary deputy. Y'all seem to talk over the evidence pretty good."

Poppa was right, even if he was joking around about me thinking Finn was cute. If Wyatt couldn't do it, I might as well see if Finn could.

"Finn." Why not? He was there. He was already helping out. He might as well stay.

Finn asked. "Are you sure you are okay?"

"Mayor." I walked up to the stage and motioned for Mayor Ryland to bend down. "What about Finn Vincent? He is already here from the Reserves and he knows the case."

The banging gavel shushed the crowd back down into their seats.

"What about a Reserve Officer?" he asked Doolittle.

She flipped and flipped some more. Finally, she looked up and shrugged.

"That's it." Mayor banged the gavel again. "I hereby appoint Finn Vincent interim Deputy Sheriff of Cottonwood."

"But..." Finn stumbled. "I can't..."

"We'll have you out of here in no time." I patted his arm and smiled.

Chapter Eighteen

"Listen up, y'all!" Jolee stood on one of the folding chairs in the back row after the council was finished voting on the new appointed deputy. Since they had called the meeting, they figured they'd discuss more of whatever it was they discussed in regular meetings. They convened for a break, giving Jolee the opportunity to sell some food.

She screamed, "I've got the truck outside so come on out and get a little pick-me-up!"

Like herds of cattle going to slaughter, everyone filed outside.

"Does she have a permit to do that?" Ben Harrison rushed up to the front of the room. "I want to file a formal complaint."

"Unfortunately, Ben..." I knew what I was about to say was not going to make him any happier. "Jolee has put in permits all over Cottonwood to be able to serve food, and Luke Jones's theatre is one of the places she's allowed."

"We aren't having movie night," Ben protested. "We're having a town meeting."

"It's not the event, it's the address." I hated to inform him because that meant no one would be hungry and head over to Ben's for after-meeting gossip and coffee.

"This is a disgrace to the community." Ben stomped, fisting his hands. "I'm going to file a complaint with Doolittle Bowman tomorrow."

"I need to talk to you." Max sidled up between Finn and me. "I found something very interesting on Ronald that I think you need to know."

"What is it?" Edna Easterly was eavesdropping.

"You field questions and I'll take this outside." I gestured between me and Max, leaving Finn to Edna Easterly, who had planted her feet firmly on the ground with her pen and paper in hand.

"Thanks," Finn groaned. "What do you want, Edna?" I heard him ask when I walked off with Max. I couldn't help but giggle. Yep, Finn was already fitting in.

Outside, Jolee's truck was packed. She had a line clear down two blocks. Everyone in Cottonwood loved to gather and eat, especially if there was gossip to be had.

Max and I walked to the side of Luke's house where we were out of earshot and sight of the food crowd. They would know we were discussing Doc Walton if they saw us, and I wasn't ready to defend my actions. Even though I didn't really need to, I always felt like I had to.

"You aren't going to believe what I found on him." Max took out his phone and showed me a picture. "I took a picture so you could see it. Do you know what that is?"

The picture was clearly of a piece of skin on Doc's body. I couldn't tell where, but the skin was clearly broken. Not from a knife, but from something else. I didn't know what.

"That's a bite mark." He poked the screen with his finger and dragged it along the wound as he explained what each part was. "This is the bruise from the teeth."

I bent down a little farther and got a good close look. Who on earth would bite an old man?

"I see it." The marks came into view like one of those pictures you have to stare at for a really long time before the squiggly lines start to make sense. "The bottom teeth are there." I pointed to four straight lines. "And the top isn't straight, the two canines really stick out."

"It's like some kind of vampire teeth." Max drew his phone away. Fear was set deep in his eyes.

"We don't have vampires in Cottonwood, or anywhere for that

matter." My eyes slid over to Jolee's truck. The crowd had died down and people were making their way back into Luke's side basement entrance.

Underneath the shadow of the big oak tree, I could see Mayor Ryland and Polly Parker in a heated discussion. They were being very careful not to be seen. Both of them looked paranoid and skittish. When someone would walk by, Polly would step back into the shadow even more as Mayor Ryland greeted the passerby who wouldn't even know Polly was there.

"I know, but this isn't the only bite." Max put the phone up to my face to get my attention back. He swiped the screen, showing another bite with a full set of straight teeth. He swiped again.

My forehead wrinkled. I took another look. I glanced back over at the tree to send Polly some bad juju, but they were gone.

I gestured for the phone and Max gave it to me. I continued to look between the two photos.

"Two different people?" The teeth were similar, but different.

"I ran a quick DNA test. They have matching DNA, which means..."

"False teeth," I interrupted. A grin crept up on my face. "Doc Walton fought off the killer after the first bite, knocking the teeth out."

"Brilliant, Kenni." Max smiled just as big as me. "I thought the same thing. I was hoping you'd come up with the same scenario."

"This means there are some false teeth somewhere out there with Doc's DNA and the killer's DNA on them." I made a mental note to go back to Doc Walton's and scour the office for a set of partials, four teeth on a dental plate.

"I took some sample tissues and sent them to the lab to run more DNA tests to see if we can find the killer's identity," Max said. "There is a specific test for saliva that I sent off to the lab."

"Great job," I said. "Finn." I called him over when I saw him turn the corner.

"There you are. Mayor Ryland asked me to find you because they're about to start the meeting again." Finn looked between Max and me. "What?" he asked. "Did you find out something on the autopsy yet?"

"I'm going back in." Max nodded toward Finn and me. "I'll let you know about that DNA test."

"DNA?" Finn looked around. He put his hand on my arm. It warmed me all over.

I backed up, allowing a moment for my heart arrhythmia to get back to normal.

"Max found bite marks on Doc." My brows furrowed. "He sent some tissue from around the marks to get DNA tested."

"Bite marks?" Finn asked. He looked down at the ground and shuffled his feet. "No offense, but that seems like a woman's move."

"No offense taken. I was thinking the same thing." The postmortem stab wounds came to mind. "Plus the stab wounds weren't deep with force." Finn's eyes lowered and a faint grin crossed his lips. "Oh." I remembered the one detail that could be important. His teeth reminded me. "False teeth. The two canines were the same but on one of the bites, the front teeth are missing."

"And he did have a lot of old people, especially women, as patients." Finn recalled the list of patients I'd given him.

"Tomorrow I plan on visiting Luke to talk to him about the tires and that movie." I snapped my fingers.

"*Summer of Sam.*" Finn smiled. I couldn't resist smiling back. "And we need to see about Viola's insurance policy."

"Since you are the low man on the totem pole," I pointed to Luke's basement, "you get to go back inside while I go home and get some much-needed sleep."

I'd had enough for one day. My stress level was through the roof and I needed Duke and my comfy bed.

I had several people to pay a visit to tomorrow, starting with Art and Wyatt at Doc's house. I needed to be in tip-top mental shape to ask Art how he fit into the circumstances of Doc Walton's murder.

Chapter Nineteen

The stress level must've really gotten to me, because I barely remembered coming home and letting Duke out to potty before I fell into my bed facedown, clothes and all. Poppa didn't make another appearance.

It took a second cup of black coffee in the morning before I could even get up off the couch and get a shower to start the new day of investigative work.

I put a couple of scoops of dog food in Duke's bowl, and with my third cup of coffee and pen and paper, I sat down in the chair and scooted it up to my table. There were people who'd caught my attention involving Doc Walton's murder and I needed to make a list. I planned on going to see each of them to try and figure out if any of them knew something, big or small, about Doc Walton and why someone would want him dead.

"Are you here, Poppa?" I looked around my kitchen, wondering if he was going to show up.

I took another sip of coffee, giving him a few minutes. I had no idea how long it took a ghost to show up. When he didn't, Duke was as good as a listener as anyone with two legs.

"Duke, how does Camille play into this?" I looked over at him. His head was down, focused on the food in his bowl. I wrote her name and underlined it. "I definitely need to pay her another visit." Beneath the line, I jotted down a few reasons I needed to see her. "For one, she and Doc Walton had a very public and heated discussion. I wonder what that was about." I bit the corner of my lip. "Plus, I'm a little curious about Polly Parker and her breakdown I heard through the wall."

I added Polly Parker to the list. Not that I thought she had anything to do with the murder, but I was curious about her.

"Then there's Viola White herself. I'm not sure she had anything to do with it. But she might have had a visitor asking questions, or maybe someone even scoped out her place and didn't see any security cameras." I wrote her name down. "But there was no forced entry."

"Don't forget the teeth marks." Poppa stood by the door. He was dressed in his brown sheriff's uniform minus the pin that was on my shirt. "You can go see Beverly Houston."

"There you are."

My heart lifted from just seeing him. I stared at him for a second. He looked great. He was healthy, not thin, and his hair was thicker than it was when he died. And his face was nice and smooth. He had a few wrinkles around the eyes, but that was it.

"I told you I was here to help you." He patted the side of his leg. Duke ran to him. "Beverly Houston." He was always good at staying on task.

"Beverly Houston because..." I stood up and paced between Poppa and the table. Duke had already taken to Poppa. "If the murderer was from Cottonwood and had false teeth, they were probably Dr. Houston's patient."

"Now you're thinking." Poppa winked.

I looked down at my list and wondered if Viola was a waste of time. I could probably talk myself out of her, but didn't. I looked down at my puny list. There wasn't much to go on. I sighed. I tapped my finger on her name.

"She might have a dental plate." Poppa shrugged. "I mean, a lot of people in town have less teeth than you think." My Poppa grinned from ear to ear. "I'm so glad you found the pin." He lifted his large wrinkled hand and pointed. "I have no idea how I lost it. I swear Max stuck it on me after he dressed me."

"Let's go." I grabbed my bag, locked the door behind us, and jumped in the Wagoneer, leaving very little time to waste. "We have a very long day ahead of us."

"Kenni! Calling all units!" Betty Murphy screamed over the walkie-talkie.

I automatically plugged my right ear with my finger and jiggled it back and forth, trying to get the high-pitched ringing from Betty's voice to go away.

"What?" I asked, immediately regretting the pissed-off tone of my voice.

"What is going on?" she asked. "The switchboard is lit up with callers saying you are zooming out of Free Row. Did something happen?"

Switchboard? There wasn't a switchboard.

"You mean call waiting?" I whispered. "I'm just driving to Doc's house to meet Art and Wyatt. There are no new crimes. And you don't need to tell anyone anything."

I assured Betty I'd be in the office after my meeting. I couldn't wait to see if Finn had gotten the ear pieces ready.

"Mornin'." Wyatt stepped out of his car after he'd met me back out on Poplar Holler Road at Doc Walton's house.

I'd left Duke in the car. He didn't need to be running around a crime scene.

"I appreciate you meeting me out here this morning." I glanced around. Poppa had gone and done his disappearing act on me again.

"You sure are making sure you cross your T's," Wyatt pointed out.

"First murder case while I've been elected, so you don't know my style." I smiled and grabbed my bag out of the Wagoneer.

"Your Poppa would be proud. He was good at investigating." Wyatt smiled and patted my back.

"I appreciate that."

I slammed the door and headed up to the house. The crime

tape was still up so anyone who tried to come would know it was an active crime scene.

"According to Toots, patients showed up at all hours of the night and sometimes Doc didn't charge them," I said. "Anyone could've come to see him and there would be no record unless he gave them a prescription."

Art's old truck rumbled up the driveway.

"What's he doing here?" Wyatt asked.

"I had him come here to show me how to use the security camera system." I waved as Art walked up to us.

"Security system?" Wyatt asked, sticking his hand out for a good ole boy shake with Art.

"That's why I told you to meet me here. Finn said that he saw some cameras on the outside of the barn." I gestured to the back of the house. "Did you know White's Jewelry didn't have a security system?"

"No," Wyatt said.

"Isn't that strange?" I wondered if her insurance company knew she didn't have a security system. Just another thing I needed to follow up on.

"Doc Walton had a security system with a camera installed on the barn." Art pointed to the building I had no idea was in use. "He had it installed when he was sure some kid was stealing his hens."

"And?" Wyatt asked.

"It was a coyote." Art laughed. "I tried to tell him it was probably an animal, but he was sure it was a teenager or something."

"Doc did have his ways." Wyatt and Art exchanged some old poker stories while I unlocked the front door and let us in.

"I'm a little freaked out to be in here." Art bit the corner of his lip and crossed his arms across his chest. "I mean, him being dead and all."

"I understand, but I need you to show me where the equipment is located and how to pull the footage." I put my hand out, squeezing his arm for some sort of comfort. "I just know it will have some evidence on there to help me bring his killer to justice."

His Adam's apple bounced up and down along with his head. I could tell he was fighting back tears.

"Can you do that for me?" I asked. "I bet Wyatt will even take you out for breakfast."

"I'm hungry too." Wyatt tapped his watch.

"Okay," Art agreed as we walked into the house. "It's in the second room on the right." He pointed down the hall behind Toots's desk. The room where Doc's life had been taken. "In the closet."

"Are you sure?" Wyatt asked.

"Positive. I'm the one who installed it." Art hung his head. "Is that where the..." He dragged his finger across his neck.

"Yes." I wasn't going to sugarcoat it. I plucked a pair of booties from the box on Toots's desk and handed him a couple to place over his shoes. "Do you think you can handle going in there?"

He didn't say a word. He just took the shoe covers and slipped them on, letting me and Wyatt lead the way.

"Be sure not to touch anything." I knew all the evidence had been collected from Finn earlier, but I still wanted to do one more sweep of the place before I turned it over to Doc's executor; I hadn't found out who that was as of yet. There had never been a time Doc talked about family. As far as I knew, he was never married or had any children.

I also gave everyone a set of gloves to put on; if the killer did know about the security system and they touched it, I didn't want to ruin any prints.

I took a deep breath before I opened the door, preparing myself for what was behind it. Even though I had seen it already, the idea of going back in wasn't high on my "want to do that again" list.

"I still can't believe Ronald had a security system," Wyatt said in disbelief. "He never said a word."

"You wouldn't believe all the people who have systems. Cameras are everywhere now." Art was looking at Wyatt when I opened the door, and then he looked inside. His jaw dropped and a small sigh escaped his open mouth like the life of him just deflated. "Who would do this?"

The splatter of blood showed the thrust of the weapon. Everything Max Bogus told me about the post-mortem stabbings was starting to make sense. I could tell the post-mortem blood splatter from the pre-mortem. The blood was darker, almost black.

"I'm hoping the camera is going to give us a little more evidence." I pointed to the ground for them to watch their steps as they trailed behind me, making our way over to the closet. "Please step over the shattered glass."

I took a quick look at where Doc had been laying when I found him. Max was right. There weren't any glass fragments near where his head had been. In fact, it was more toward his feet. Was Max's theory right about the mercury globules? If that was the case, was Doc Walton's death premeditated or was it spontaneous?

I turned my attention toward the closet door Wyatt and Art had just opened.

Art was right. I was not expecting to see what was behind the door. The security system was state of the art. There were so many black boxes with chasing lights, blinking lights, and lights that stayed on.

"Wow." Wyatt leaned closer to get a good look. "You do all this stuff?"

"Yeah." It was Art's opening to brag on himself. He went on and on about how technology had come a long way in just a few years and Doc wanted something that was going to penetrate through the dark night since he lived in the country and there wasn't light other than the moon. He pointed to the little TV and told us Doc could watch live if he wanted to. "Here's the chip." Art pushed a button and out popped a little microchip.

I pulled an evidence baggie out of my bag as Wyatt stuck his hand out.

"In here." I thrust the bag in front of his hand. "Just in case."

Art dropped the microchip in the bag and I closed it up, using my pen to write "Evidence" on it.

"Thank you, Art." I held the bag close to me. "You have no idea how much this will help in figuring out who did this."

Art turned away from the closet. "I hope so, but if he didn't roll back the times..."

"Roll back the times?" I asked.

"Ronald didn't want the continuous feed. He wanted to watch it night by night. When he found out it was coyotes and fixed the problem, he mentioned during poker night that he didn't really use the system much anymore." A sadness drew down his thin face, making his cheeks droop more.

"Let's just hope." I patted him on the back and pointed toward the door.

When we all were back out in the hallway, I shut the door and led them to the front porch. The sun was still shining, which was a good thing since the town council decided to let the festival continue.

If the rain stayed away for the rest of the night and the next few days, the muddy mess at the fairgrounds would be able to hold the carnival equipment coming to town in a couple days to set up. That would be good news for Cottonwood. We needed a little reprieve from all the bad news we'd been given.

"Art," I stopped him before he left. He turned around. "I understand that Viola White had an appointment with you and cancelled it."

"She did," he confirmed.

"Do you find it strange that she didn't have cameras installed at the jewelry store?" I was no expert on who did or who didn't have cameras and why they wouldn't, but I was curious to see his thoughts.

"I've been on Viola for years now." He shook his head. "She's so hard headed. She claims that if someone wants to steal something bad enough, security cameras aren't going to keep them away." He laughed. "I told her security cameras weren't to keep them away; they were to catch the robbers in the act. She just couldn't get that concept."

Art and I said goodbye. I walked away to let him and Wyatt make their breakfast plans.

"Fresh eyes, Kenni-bug." Poppa danced around the car and into the passenger seat. "Sometimes deep secrets in a small town are hidden from us. Fresh eyes can see those secrets. Most of the time, secrets have a way of revealing themselves."

I looked at Poppa, figuring he must've meant Finn.

"Kenni?" Wyatt asked. I hadn't seen him come over.

"Yeah, yeah." I shook my head, coming back to the present.

"Are you okay?" Wyatt asked. His excited tone turned to concern.

"Yes. I was just thinking about Doc Walton and how brutal this all was. And for what?" My thoughts came out of my mouth.

"I recognize that pin." Wyatt smiled, his eyes on the lapel of my brown sheriff shirt.

I ran the pad of my finger over it and couldn't stop the smile on my face.

"I found it in my Wagoneer." I glanced over at the old car my Poppa had given me and him sitting up front. "I swear I've cleaned that old thing inside and out several times since he passed and I'd never seen it."

"I thought they buried it with him." Wyatt's shoulders jumped when he let out a little laugh. "I swear I saw it on him in the coffin before they closed it and we carried him out to the hearse."

"Really?" I asked, trying to recall, but I had blocked out most of the funeral out of grief.

Wyatt had been a pallbearer. He was close with Poppa.

"Maybe it was a different one." Wyatt shrugged again. "I guess I better get going. Art is probably halfway to town by now."

"I'll see you in an hour or so." I waved and jumped in the front of the Wagoneer. I quickly rolled down the window. "Hey." I stopped him before he got into his car. "Max told me something that makes me sick."

"What was that?" Wyatt rested his hand on the top of his open driver's door.

"He said that most of the stab wounds were post-mortem and Doc probably didn't die from being stabbed." Images of some raging figure stabbing Doc's dead body played in my head like one of Luke Jones's movies.

"Oh my God." Wyatt ran his hands through his hair.

"It seems like someone was really angry with Doc." The crease between my brows deepened.

"That is sick." Wyatt's mouth opened, his eyes closed. "Who would do such a thing?"

"Someone who was very angry." I held the baggie up. "And I hope their car or something is on this microchip."

"Do you want me to file that as evidence?" Wyatt asked.

"That would be great. Be sure to log it first." I handed him the baggie.

"What does Max think killed him?" Wyatt asked, shaking his head and looking down at his feet.

"Mercury poisoning." My skin crawled at the thought of it.

"Mercury poisoning?" Wyatt grimaced.

"Yeah. Like the mercury from a broken thermometer." I brushed my fingers over my lip. "There were granules embedded in his mustache and a broken thermometer at the scene. The way his body was laying it was not possible for him to fall face first into the mercury from the broken thermometer."

"We are going to nail the sick bastard," Wyatt spat. Anger flared in his eyes.

"Yes, we are," I confirmed.

Chapter Twenty

It was still early for me to go around knocking on doors and questioning people. The one person I knew that was up and probably having breakfast at Cowboy's Catfish was Katy Lee Hart. She ran her family's insurance business, Hart Insurance. I had a good hankerin' that she'd know if Viola White had an insurance policy on the jewelry store.

Cowboy's Catfish had the usual crowd ready for grits and gravy. Betty was sitting at the counter with the cordless phone in hand, sipping her coffee and talking to the regulars. We nodded at each other.

"Kenni!" Tibbie Bell waved me and Duke over to her table.

I tried not to make eye contact with anyone else as I made my way through the tables, but I could feel the stares and hushed talk when I walked by.

"I was going to call you last night, but I figured your hands were full." Tibbie pushed the chair next to her out for me to sit between her and Katy Lee.

I raised my hand when I saw Bartleby glance my way. He gave a slight nod in acknowledgment. It was our unspoken signal that I needed a coffee and he needed to open the door between the jail and restaurant so Duke could go back there. I sat down and put my police bag on the ground and let go of Duke's leash.

I watched him make his way around the tables with his nose to the ground, sucking up any food that had made its way on the floor, before he disappeared into the door leading to the back of the jail.

"Rowdy told me he's seen you at the cemetery a lot lately." Katy Lee patted my hand.

Katy Lee was a little thick around the waist, but fashionable to the hilt. Her blond hair was always parted to the side and curled in long loose tendrils. Besides the family insurance business, she sold Shabby Trends, a line of expensive clothing, on the side. Shabby Trends was like Tupperware. The only way to purchase the clothes was to have home parties and the clothes were just seasonal. It was kind of nice since someone couldn't buy the skirt I'd bought from her a year ago. Today she had on a cute button-front dress with large yellow stripes and her cowboy boots.

Tibbie leaned in, her stare drilling into me, waiting for my reply to what Katy Lee had said.

Tibbie's long brown hair was straight and parted down the middle, hanging over one shoulder and falling down to her waist. Her Ray-Ban sunglasses acted like a headband on top of her head. She too had on a dress, solid green with a big brown belt around her thin waist. She had on boots too, but hers zipped up the back and were taller than Katy's.

"Thank you," I whispered when Bartleby put the cup down in front of me.

"Do you want something to eat?" he asked.

"No. I need to go back to the office." I gestured to the back of the restaurant. Bartleby rushed off to the register, where there was a line for people to pay their bill.

"Seriously, tell us how you're holding up," Tibbie said. Her skin tone and hazel eyes really stood out against the green dress. It was natural for my good friends to ask me about my life, but I knew they also wanted the lowdown on the investigation.

"I'm fine. A little busy, that's all." I carefully pulled the cup up to my lips and blew on the hot liquid, nearly choking on the substance when Poppa appeared next to the table. We were going to have to have a signal, like a ringing of a bell or something, to alert me that he was about to make an appearance.

"Kenni?" Katy Lee's eyes slid to the space I was staring into.

"What are you staring at?"

"Nothing. I was just thinking about something with the case," I lied, hoping they would just drop it.

"Are you sure you're okay?" Katy Lee leaned forward on the table, resting on her forearms. "I didn't want to say anything, but Rowdy told me that you were talking to yourself and someone heard you were seen going into Dr. Shively's office."

I shook my head. "I'm fine," I blew it off. "I have a bad habit of talking to Poppa's stone as if he's there. I just had a couple medical questions for Camille."

"Let's go. We need to make sure the evidence got sent to the crime lab, Kenni-bug." Poppa bent down near Tibbie's head trying to get my attention.

"I've got to go to the office." I stood up, grabbed my bag, and picked up the mug. "I'll see you tonight at Euchre." My chair scooted across the floor when I stood up. "Katy Lee, I'll be stopping by your office this morning." I wanted to make sure she knew I was coming. I couldn't openly talk to her here.

"Sure." Katy Lee's eyes popped open wide and she drew back in suspicion. "You know where to find me."

We said our goodbyes. Before I turned the corner of the diner to head back to the office, I glanced back at my friends. Their heads were huddled together and there was no doubt in my mind that they were coming up with all sorts of stories for why I was going to stop by the insurance agency.

"You have got to stop showing up like that without warning." I put the bag on my desk and looked at my Poppa.

Duke had laid down on the big pillow bed behind my desk and was snoring loudly.

"Going around having coffee with friends isn't going to solve the crimes." He pointed his finger toward the restaurant. "All of those people in there eating are watching you. Especially now that you have to step up and get a killer behind bars." His gestures were exactly how Poppa would act alive. I had seen him give a similar speech to Wyatt when they were working on a crime spree that spread across the entire state. "I'm not saying ignore your friends. Do your job, then socialize." He lifted his hands in the air.

"I can't go around ignoring everyone in town. It's so small, I see my friends everywhere." I brought up my email, hitting print when I saw the tire photos from Finn. "Plus Katy Lee would have information on any insurance policy Viola might have."

"Good thinking, Kenni-bug." Poppa tapped his noggin with his finger. "Keep your ear to the ground and hear the gossip. Some of my best investigative work was going to Stella's Bible study." Poppa followed me over to the printer.

"How so?" I asked, taking a good look at the tire marks.

"Those women don't spend too much time around the Bible. They spend time eating and gossiping. You wouldn't believe what you find out just by listening." He glanced over my shoulder at the photo.

I held it up so he could get a better view.

"Here are the tire tracks that had dried perfectly in the mud." I pointed out the tracks. "I looked in the front yard the morning of the murder, but it was so muddy from the rain. It is possible the killer drove to the back of the house and parked."

"You're on the right track." Poppa smiled, pride on his face.

"Do you know who did it?" I asked, hoping he'd tell me if he did.

"No. I told you that." His voice cracked. He shook his head. He continued, "I was trying to keep the town safe. I failed you, Kenni-bug."

"You didn't fail me." Suddenly talking to Poppa's ghost didn't feel so strange. "Now you can help me." I gulped back tears, letting go of the fact that I might be seeing things because talking to him made me feel so much better.

This was far better than going to the cemetery and talking to his stone.

"Like you said, if anyone knows about tires, it's Luke." I shook the photo. Luke not only had the basement theatre, he owned Pump and Munch, the gas station in the middle of town. Luke was a mechanic and he knew his stuff. "And I'm going to ask him about *Summer of Sam.*"

"*Summer of Sam?*" Wyatt stood in the doorway. He glanced around the small room. "Do you have someone in the holding room?"

"No." I pulled the photo down to my chest.

"Who are you talking to?" His wiry brows furrowed.

"Duke." I laughed nervously. Duke lifted his head. "I think better out loud." I walked over to Wyatt. "Look at this."

He took the photo from my hand.

"What is it?" he asked.

Poppa stood over Wyatt's shoulder looking at the photo. Duke jumped up and ran to Poppa's side. Poppa rubbed Duke's head. Duke rolled his head in the air, taking advantage of all of Poppa's fingers.

"What's wrong with him?" Wyatt's mouth clenched. He shifted to his right and turned his head to get a look behind him at Duke.

Crap.

Duke did look a little silly, flailing his head in the air, and since Wyatt couldn't see Poppa, Duke looked like he was having some sort of seizure.

"Duke." I got his attention and Poppa's. "What are you doing?" My voice cracked as I tried to get Poppa's attention to stop petting the dog. "Go lay down."

Poppa flicked his hand trying to brush Duke away, but Duke was having none of it. He jumped around on his hind legs, bouncing back and forth like he did when Poppa played with him.

"Are you sure he's okay? It's like he sees something." Wyatt looked at the space where Poppa was standing. "You know," Wyatt scratched his head, "he used to act like that around Elmer," he mused, using my Poppa's name.

"Maybe he's hungry." I walked back over to my desk and opened the bottom drawer where I kept extra dog food for when I was at the office. I dumped a handful into the bowl next to his bed. "Here, Duke!"

Playtime was over when it came to food. Duke ran over to the bowl, completely forgetting about Poppa, gobbling up the kibble.

I walked back over to Wyatt and shoved the photo back in his face.

"Those are tire tracks from the back of Doc Walton's house." I pointed them out. "Finn took them. I meant to show those to you this morning, but I wanted us to get to the bottom of the security cameras."

"What does this prove?" Wyatt looked at me.

"Well..." I looked at the photos again. "It really doesn't prove anything right now, but it might tie in somewhere," I said. "Finn found them while securing Doc's office. He also said there were smudged mud marks by the door where someone had tried to wipe off footprints." I smiled, remembering what Toots had said about Doc Walton hating muddy feet and how he made clients take off their shoes.

Wyatt snapped his fingers in the air and said, "Doc Walton didn't let anyone come in his home with their shoes on. The killer probably knew it and came in the back, then tried to smudge their shoe prints, which would have been evidence if we found out what type of shoes the killer had on."

"But," I poked the photo with my finger, "we have better. Tire marks. And I'm going to ask Luke what type of tires these are and see what car uses this type of tire."

"A good start since we don't have a lot of leads," Wyatt acknowledged. "But don't get your hopes up. Nowadays, all cars can use the same brand of tire."

"It might be a long shot, but I'm not going to look at it that way. It could be a clue."

I wasn't going to let Wyatt burst my bubble. I was going to check all the evidence. Twice if I had to.

"Attagirl." Poppa stood behind Wyatt, tapping his temple. "Using your noggin just like your old Poppa."

"I thought I told you to send this off for evidence." I pointed to some of the files on his desk that had the information on possible fingerprints picked up at the scene along with the gloves Doc had and different blood samples.

"Ran out of time yesterday. I'll get those off right now." Wyatt took the bag with the microchip. "And I'll send this off with the rest." He looked up at me and smiled. "If I didn't know better, I would think I was standing here with Sheriff Elmer." He tapped his finger on the desk between us. "You are starting to think like him. Good job, Sheriff."

I smiled, taking all the credit. Poppa winked.

"When I walked in you said *Summer of Sam*." Wyatt pulled out the evidence bags and log where we tracked evidence that needed to be sent off. A sheet we never had used before.

"Have you seen the movie?" I asked.

"You didn't have to see the movie to know about it. It was a big case. National attention." Wyatt scribbled on the log and pulled the back off the envelope to seal it.

I pulled the camera out of my bag and walked over to Wyatt's desk.

"This is Doc's wrist." I showed him the Sharpie tattoo.

"Ronald had a tattoo?" Wyatt's face contorted.

"No." I pushed the forward button and showed him the carpet from White's. "This was spray-painted on the carpet at White's. Tying both crimes together. The killer wants us to know they are connected."

"What the hell is it?" he asked, then apologized for his language.

I clicked the forward button on the camera again to show him the photo on Kim's Buffet's wall. "I went over to Kim's and asked Mrs. Kim what this was because I knew it was some sort of Chinese symbol."

"And?" he coaxed me.

"She said it meant 'family.'"

"Ronald didn't have any family around here." Wyatt didn't tell me anything I didn't already know. "So what does this mean?"

"I don't know. I want you to look into getting his will, calling next of kin and all of that. I'm hoping we come up with some names and talk to them. Did he ever talk about his family?"

"Never." He shook his head. "But I'm not following the Son of Sam thing."

"Me neither, but I heard that killer left behind notes or markings or something and it just didn't sit well in my gut." I put my hand on my stomach. It was growling; time for me to grab something to eat. "What about teeth marks?"

"Teeth marks?"

Wyatt stared at me, baffled.

"Doc Walton had two sets of bite marks on him." The words made my stomach curl. Who on earth could have done this to him? "I'm thinking the killer bit Doc while Doc fought them off and the killer had some sort of partial that Doc knocked out of their mouth."

Wyatt's face contorted. "I think you're going to solve these crimes. Where is Officer Vincent?"

"Yes, I am. I'm not sure where he is this morning." I looked at my watch. It was still pretty early and I hadn't told him a specific time to get to the office. "I imagine he had some calls to make to the Reserves about him taking the part-time deputy position."

"It's good to have him onboard. He seems very thorough. I'm just sorry I wasn't able to take the position." The corners of his eyes sagged. "I feel like you're investigating like your Poppa and it sure would've been fun solving some crimes with you."

"You are." I patted the evidence bag. "You're helping me out more than you know."

I really wasn't sure why he hadn't sent off the evidence we had collected the day of the murder yet. It was of the upmost importance. All law enforcement knew that the first forty-eight hours in a murder case was the most important. The longer time went on, the harder it was to solve a crime. I wasn't about to let my first murder case become a cold case. But I decided to let Wyatt off the hook. He was only looking out for me. After all, he'd been around my whole life.

"Anything new, gang?" Betty sashayed in, the phone tucked under her armpit and her coffee in her hands.

I grabbed the form I needed to get a warrant. If I gave it to Betty now, she'd be able to get it down to the courthouse and in front of the judge by day's end.

"Betty, I'm filling out this warrant request to get my hands on Camille Shively's files." I signed the form and handed it to her. "Can you get this over to the judge ASAP while Wyatt sends off the evidence? I need to go interview a couple of more people."

"I sure will." She put the phone on the charger and took the paper. "Do you think she had anything to do with it?"

"I don't know. But they were in public discussing something in a very heated manner and she's not saying much to me right now." I knew the warrant would speak volumes.

"I'll keep my ear to the ground with the women in my sewing circle. They always have some good gossip about rumblings," Betty noted and went on to fill out the paperwork.

Chapter Twenty-One

I left Duke at the jail. It wasn't like he wanted to come with me anyway. His belly was full and he was happily sleeping on his big pillow Ruby Smith had gotten from one of the estate sales she had attended. Today I had a lot of stops to make and leaving him in the car wasn't something he would want. Wyatt said he'd be at the office working and he'd let Duke out to potty and make sure he had plenty of water.

Duke liked Wyatt. Wyatt was known to take Duke on little trips with him. Everyone liked Duke. His name even made it on a write-in ballot against Mayor Ryland in the last election. Something the mayor wasn't too happy about. I had no idea who had written Duke in, but I loved the idea.

"Where to now?" Poppa rubbed his hands together in the front seat.

"Well, I am going to go see Beverly Houston, Katy Lee, and Luke Jones," I said without looking at my list. That should take up my day until I had to be at my weekly Euchre game.

Beverly Houston's dental office was located on the north side of town past Lulu's Boutique in a little strip mall. Jolee's food truck was once again set up along the side of the boutique and the line was down the street.

I did a double take and gripped the wheel when I saw Finn in the front of the line. I turned down the street, pulled in front of the food truck, put my hazards on, and got out.

"Are you cutting line?" Finn nudged me. He had on a solid t-shirt, jeans, the same big belt buckle, and now a pair of cowboy boots.

"One day in Cottonwood and we turned this Yank into a country boy." Jolee winked from behind the window. "The usual?"

"Nah." I waved her off. "I'm not staying. Give him the usual."

He shook his head. "I'm going to have country ham biscuit with a dollop of gravy and eggs sunny-side up. A little oozy, but a whole lot of goodness." He grinned. I momentarily lost all sense of what I was doing there. "I think those were your exact words."

Jolee cocked her head to the side. "And to think I wasn't gonna raise my hand last night to vote you in as deputy. Shame on me." She winked and went back to making his order.

"No food?" he asked. We stepped to the side so the others could order.

"I already had enough coffee for everyone in this line," I joked. "I'm going to go to the dentist's office to show Beverly Houston those teeth marks and see what I can find out. I already told Katy Lee Hart I'd be by to talk to her. She's the insurance agent in Cottonwood. She'd know if Viola would've had insurance on the store."

"Sounds good. What if I grab my breakfast and meet you at Hart's?" he asked.

"You know, I hadn't thought of that, but it's a good idea." I snapped my fingers. "Two heads are better than one."

"Maybe." He laughed. His smile reached his eyes and my heart thumped a little too hard.

"I'll see you in a little bit." I left before I couldn't hide the awkward attraction I was feeling for him.

I'd head on over to Beverly Houston's office first. That would give him plenty of time to eat and give me enough time to feel out Beverly.

Within a couple of minutes, I was sitting in Beverly's parking lot glancing in the rearview mirror. I liked to get a good view of my surroundings. The strip mall had the dentist's office, Tiny Tina's, The Pawn, Cottonwood Federal Savings, Hart's insurance office, and a Subway. A few of the rockers that lined the front of the strip mall shops were occupied by customers. They were probably waiting for their turn at Dr. Houston's.

Katy Lee didn't look like she was at the insurance office yet, which meant she was probably still sitting with Tibbie at Cowboy's Catfish.

I got out and headed into Dr. Houston's office.

The smell of fluoride and the buzzing sound of some sort of drill made the hairs on my arms stand to attention. The only thing that really scared me was the dentist. Not even the thought of Poppa's ghost scared me as much as standing where I was at this moment.

"Hi." I smiled at the receptionist. "I'm here on official business to see Beverly Houston."

The receptionist's eyes popped when she looked up and noticed my sheriff's uniform. She gave a quick nod and scurried out of the office. The sound of the drill stopped and a few whispers floated through the hall, followed by the sound of footsteps.

Beverly Houston appeared with the receptionist in the office. Her curly brown hair was pulled back in a low ponytail and a blue mask dangled from a string off her left ear. She wore blue scrubs and blue latex gloves.

"Sheriff." She tossed the gloves in the trash and stuck her hand out. We did the official business shake. "You can come back here." She nodded for me to follow her back to her office.

"Ding, ding." Poppa stood by the door of her office pretending to shake invisible bells. "My presence is known."

I glared at him. He was always good at making smart-aleck remarks and making me giggle. Then again, I was never at the butt of his jokes until now.

"She sure is smart." Poppa looked at all the framed diplomas hanging on the walls. I did my best to ignore him and keep a poker face.

"It's good to see you." Beverly smiled. She was ten years older than me and I really didn't know much about her. Other than seeing her every six months for a cleaning, I steered clear of her. She wasn't the prettiest of women in Cottonwood, nor the ugliest. She was just average, with a little more girth around her stomach. "I understand you are here on official business." She tucked a loose strand of hair back into the low ponytail at the nape of her neck.

Her hair was brown with natural curl and a little dry. She could stand to get a hot oil treatment from Tiny Tina. I wondered if I should give her my prescription from Camille. I had never seen Dr. Houston do anything to her hair other than the low ponytail. Her bangs hung to her brow in waves. She pushed them out of her face. She could have used a good consult from Katy Lee in the clothing department too.

"Yes." I pulled out the camera from my bag. "I'm not sure how you can help me." I flipped the camera on. "But I just knew I needed to see you when I got this lead in the Doctor Ronald Walton case."

"Is that about his murder?" she asked, easing down into the chair behind her desk. "It's awful. Just awful." Sympathy hung on her words, her head dipped.

"Actually, murderer." I took a step forward, the photo screen on the camera held out for her to see.

"I'm sorry, Doctor." The receptionist stood at the door with Finn Vincent towering over her shoulder. "Officer Vincent said he's with Sheriff Lowry."

"Excuse me." Finn moved around the receptionist and walked into the office. "I ate in my car on the way over, so I hope you don't mind me joining."

"Not at all." I encouraged him to come on in. He was definitely a sight I could get used to looking at first thing in the morning. "Officer Vincent, this is Doctor Houston." They greeted each other. I watched how he handled getting to know new people and how at ease he was.

"I was just about to show her the bite pictures." I put the camera on the desk.

Beverly's eyes grazed over Finn. She smiled. She ignored the camera and stood up, straightened her shoulders, took the dangling mask off her ear and threw her hand out in front of her. "Your teeth are amazing."

"Thank you. My parents would be happy with your comment." He smiled. She was right. His teeth were just the icing on his cake. I gulped.

"You have a thing for him." Poppa stood next to Beverly with his mouth gaped open. "Kendrick Lowry! Do you?" Poppa asked, like I was going to answer him right then and there.

I swallowed hard.

"I heard about the meeting last night. Congratulations on your new post." She dropped his hand and went back behind her desk.

"Thank you. I'm happy to be here to assist Sheriff Lowry." He took a seat next to mine.

"I'd love to take a look in that mouth of yours." Beverly's head darted back and forth, trying to get a look into his mouth.

"If I'm still in town when I need my next cleaning, you can take all the time you need." His words sounded more seductive than official. A brief shiver rippled through me and my brain seemed to freeze.

Beverly and I both stood there, in a daze.

"Kenni-bug." Poppa clapped his hands. I jumped and focused on the task at hand.

"How can I help you?" Beverly sat down in her desk and folded her hands neatly on the top.

I flipped the camera back on and shoved it toward her. "This has to do with Doc Walton's death. Max Bogus found two sets of bite marks on him. One has teeth marks all the way across and the other seems to be missing teeth."

Beverly looked at the camera.

"I was wondering if you could tell if they came from the same mouth." I pushed the button to forward the frame to the next picture. Even though I already knew it was one person, I was curious to see if she came to the same conclusion as I had or if she would recognize the dental work or patient. "I don't know anything about teeth and I couldn't tell you what these are called. But I'm thinking by the size of the bite, the distance between the teeth, you could tell me in your professional opinion if they're from the same mouth."

"Do you agree these aren't the same bite marks?" Finn drew back and squinted like he was trying to get a different angle.

"I'm wondering if there was a dental plate, and after the first bite Doc Walton flailed or fought back, knocking the killer's teeth out." It was a long shot, but it was all I had to go on. And it seemed pretty reasonable.

She gestured her finger. "Go back." She squinted before she held her hand out. "May I?" She wanted to hold the camera.

"Only these two photos." I made sure she knew not to flip through anymore.

"Why don't I hold it while you take a good look?" Finn took the camera from me, walked around Beverly's desk and held it close to her face. "Here is the full bite set." Her head bent down a little. "Here is the other one."

I watched her intently. Her chest slowly moved up and down, her face paled, she swallowed hard, and she closed her eyes for a long second.

"This one is missing the front two teeth, which makes it look like two different people. Go back." Her voice trembled. Closing her eyes must've helped her gather her wits about her because her voice sounded stronger. "Really, it's one person."

"How do you know?" I asked.

"In the first one with all the teeth, the canine on the right side has a chip out of it." She pointed to the tooth she was talking about. "Next one," she ordered Finn. "This canine has the same chip out, which tells me the other bite was first because this person does wear a dental appliance."

"So it is possible Doctor Walton hit the person, knocking out the appliance, but the person bit again?" Finn asked, painting a picture of how the killer could've possibly lost his teeth.

"In my professional opinion, that is very much possible."

She smiled, pleased with her analysis.

"What type of dental appliance?" I asked.

"Probably a partial denture. Nothing too terribly exciting." She shrugged. "You see these types of partials in older people."

"Older people," I repeated.

"Can you give us a list of patients who have partials?" Finn asked.

"I can't do that." Beverly pushed her chair back. Her face had gained a little bit of color back in her cheeks. "I'm sworn to client confidentiality. That whole HIPAA law thing. Plus, you don't have a warrant, do you?"

"No," I chimed in. "I was hoping I wouldn't have to bother the judge for that and you'd comply with us."

Something told me Beverly knew someone with this same kind of partial and chip on their canine, but she had buttoned up on me.

"You do want to help us find the killer and get him or her off the streets of Cottonwood, right?" Finn smiled, his teeth gleaming.

"Of course I do." She grabbed the mask off of her desk, avoiding eye contact. "But I have a life to live and if there is no warrant...The law is the law and I have bills to pay. I can't help you any further." She put the stretchy straps around each ear. "Excuse me." She walked past us, putting the mask over her mouth. "You know the way out," she said in a muffled voice.

With tucked tails, Finn and I walked out of the office, but not without the eyes of the receptionist and a couple of patients watching us.

"That didn't go as planned." Finn stopped outside, rocking back on his heels.

"Oh, I don't know." I turned toward him. The sky was blue. Hopefully the sun would stay out and help dry out the fairgrounds even more. "I think it helped narrow down Doc's patient files. And with a warrant, we can cross check them."

I looked around for Poppa, but his ghost wasn't there.

Finn slid his aviators out of the front pocket of his shirt and slipped them on his face.

"I..." I hesitated and looked away. He looked so hot in those glasses, it was hard to concentrate on being a badass sheriff. It bugged me that I found him disturbingly attractive. So much so that I was getting angry with myself.

"I think we need to go see Katy Lee now."

"I'm here to help." He took a few steps forward, turning to face the strip mall. He looked to the left, and then to the right. "That's the insurance company you said White's Jewelry held their policy?" Finn asked, and took a step toward Katy Lee's office.

"It is." I followed behind him.

"Listen." Finn ran his hand through his hair and let out a deep sigh. Oh, how I wished he didn't do that. His charm confused me. "Are you going to get a warrant or not? I'm sure you can just push in that button," he plucked the walkie-talkie from my shoulder, "and call in the warrant. You need it for that patient list you were talking about." He pointed to Beverly's office.

"She went completely silent and pale. She knows something." There had to be a way to get the patient list without going for the warrant. But how? "Let me see if I can get her to change her mind at Euchre."

"Euchre?" Finn let out another sigh, longer this time, as though he was losing his mind.

"What?" I asked, snarling.

"I feel like I'm fighting a losing battle. When I say get a warrant, I mean now." He threw his hands in the air. "Not next week. Now is the time to solve the murder. The first couple of days in a murder case are the most crucial and you think you can sweet-talk her over a hand of Euchre?"

"No, but the power of the other women can be better than a warrant."

I knew I was right. The Euchre women had a way of getting others to do what needed to be done and I was confident I would have the list later tonight.

"You seem a little off today." His eyes lowered. "I think Jolee was right." He laughed and shook his head. "She warned me. She said you were pretty private, but I thought you were a lot more professional than that. I guess you aren't like your Poppa."

"Listen here." I grabbed his arm, bringing him closer to me. He towered over me, his face bent down, nose to nose. I curled up on my toes, my nails still dug in his arm. Being this close to him was almost too much. I couldn't decide whether I wanted to smack him or kiss him. His arresting good looks captivated me, but I had to keep a clear head.

"You don't know a thing about my Poppa." I pushed his arm away from me, trying to get him to back away, but he wasn't moving. His smell made me dizzy. I clenched my teeth, my jaw tensed. The air leaving his nose breezed across my lips. "You leave him out of this." I had to take a step back in fear of him hearing my rapidly beating heart.

"Fine," he said in a whisper, sticking his hands in the air, taking a step back. "The way I see it..." The edges of Finn's lips tipped up. Poppa appeared next to him. He continued, "You've spent all your life trying to make your Poppa proud, and from what I hear he worked well with his deputy. I get that you've had Lonnie for the past two years to drink coffee with and not solve crimes, but you've got to get on the ball and follow up on these leads. Euchre, gossiping women or not, you need a warrant."

He brought the walkie-talkie that was still in his hand and still tethered to me up to his mouth. "Betty, it's Finn."

"Finn? Where's Kenni?" Betty questioned. "Don't tell me something happened to her."

"Nothing like that. She's here with me. We need you to fill out a form for a warrant for Doctor Beverly Houston's patient files," he said.

I grabbed my walkie-talkie.

"Betty." I glared at him. "Please take it down to the courthouse ASAP."

"I just got back from there filing Camille's warrant. You got any more so we can save time?" she snarked.

The glass door of Katy Lee's office swung open.

"Well, you might as well fill one out for Hart Insurance too." I took my finger off the button and Velcroed it back on my shoulder.

"Kenni?" Katy Lee stuck her head out of the open door. "What are you doing?"

I gulped, swallowing my pride. As much as I wanted to punch Officer Vincent in his gorgeous face, he was right. I was going to have to go with the law and not rely on a little gossip and Euchre.

"You'll be a hero if you solve the case," Poppa said. "He's right. It takes an army to fight crime, Kenni-bug. You have the brains, he's the brawn." Poppa put his scrawny arms in the air, making muscle poses. "You two could make quite the pair."

I laughed out loud.

"Kenni?" Katy Lee stepped out on the sidewalk of the strip mall.

I bent over in a fit of giggles and placed a hand on one of the rockers before I sat down in it. I looked crazy and I knew it.

Chapter Twenty-Two

"What was that about?" Katy Lee asked me once we got into her office.

She and I stood by her coffee maker filling up three cups with her fresh brewed coffee. The space was one large room with an emphasis on cozy. There was a large cream-colored fuzzy rug in the middle of the room, surrounded by a couch, coffee tables, and two end chairs. I was sure they used this room to sign clients up. Katy Lee had a knack for making everyone feel welcome.

Sometimes she used the space for her sample sales of Shabby Trends. It was a lot of fun to get together with girlfriends, eat, and try on fun clothes.

"Nothing." I couldn't stop smiling. Poppa had me tickled like he used to do when I was a child and pouting. He always knew how to bring me out of a hissy fit. "I think Finn might be making me crazy." I poured powder creamer into my cup.

"Because you have to be around him and be professional?" She wiggled her brows up and down. She leaned over and whispered, "He's so hot."

I nudged her with my elbow.

"What? Did you smell him?" She moaned and let out a happy sigh. "No wonder you seem to be dragging your feet on this investigation." She smiled.

"Who said that?" I jerked back, irritated. "I'm doing no such thing."

"Relax. Geez." She picked up her coffee and Finn's. She arranged them on a white wooden tray along with a few cookies on a plate and carried it all over to the sitting area, but not before saying, "Maybe you do need a good romp in the sack with him. You're testy."

She flipped her head, her hair swinging behind her shoulder, and sashayed her way back to Finn. She sat the tray on the coffee table and gestured for Finn to take a seat.

"It's nice to see a friendly face around here." Finn gave me a quick look before he took a drink from the tray and sat down.

"I'm friendly," I groaned. "Katy Lee and I have been friends a long time and I know she'll help us without a warrant. Right, Katy Lee?"

"Right." She blew on her coffee and eased down in one of the chairs. I sat in the other. "Wait. Help with what?"

"We're investigating the break-in at White's." Finn didn't tell her all the details. I was glad he stuck to just the break-in. "We're looking into all possible suspects, and we know Ms. White keeps an insurance policy on her property with you and your business."

"Are you telling me that you think Viola killed Doc and broke into her own business?"

I planted my palm on my head. "No, no, no. The two probably aren't related."

Katy Lee might be one of my best friends, but any information about the cases was off limits to anyone in Cottonwood. No one could keep his or her mouth shut. No one.

"We are investigating one crime at a time. We need to see Viola's insurance policy. Police procedure." I had to clear up the big spill, but knew she wasn't buying it. There was no way I was going to tell her about the Chinese symbol and how it connected the two crimes.

Her eyes lowered, her long lashes creating a shadow on her cheeks. She smiled.

"You're going to have to give me more than that if you want me to just hand it over." She crossed her legs and leaned back in the chair.

"We don't have a reason she'd kill the doctor, but insurance is a good reason to break into your own business. And there wasn't any clear point of break-in. It was like someone had a key." Finn continued to flap jaw and spill the beans.

He had so much to learn about small towns and gossip. I looked at him under furrowed brows.

My mouth dropped.

"What?" He shrugged. "Sometimes you have to be straight up."

"Yeah, Kenni." Katy Lee laughed. "It is true Viola keeps her insurance with us, but she only insures the jewelry since she doesn't own the building." Katy Lee stood up and walked over to the big gray filing cabinet across the room, near the "office" area of the room. There were two desks, one for her and one for her dad. She ran her finger down the front of the cabinet and jerked one of the bottom drawers open, sliding it to full extension.

My eyes popped and I looked at Finn. He reacted to my shock by smiling. He was right. If Viola was in trouble, it wouldn't be beneath her to make an insurance claim. But she wasn't a killer. Was she?

Katy pulled out a file that was two inches thick.

"Of course, this remains confidential."

She gave Finn a look.

"Of course." Finn's brows formed a V as he took the file.

"You can see here that Viola has had this policy with us," Katy Lee put her hand on her chest, "for years."

She walked back over and sat down next to Finn on the couch. She was practically sitting in his lap. She sucked in a deep breath, letting a grin travel across her lips. She wasn't fooling me. She was taking a nice long whiff of Finn's smell.

"She keeps large policies on the merchandise. Especially this one." She plucked a piece of paper from the stack. "This diamond in her store is worth every bit of two million dollars." She smacked the paper down on Finn's lap. "I tried to tell her and my daddy tried to tell her not to keep such a big piece of jewelry in the shop, especially in Cottonwood." She smacked his arm and giggled. "Because we all know no one in this Podunk town is going to buy it." She jerked around to me with a stunned look on her face. "Oh my God. Did they steal the diamond?"

"I had Wyatt take Viola's statement and inventory. I don't know yet. We're just trying to see if there's a reason she would break into her own shop." I took the picture Katy Lee had and snapped a quick picture of it with my phone.

"She didn't own the shop." Poppa appeared in the back of the insurance office and stared over at us. "Who owned it?"

I smacked my hands together. "Do you have the building owner's insurance?" I asked.

"We do...ohmyGod!" Katy Lee's words ran together. "And the owner had approached us about selling and said that he wasn't going to sell it to Viola White."

"Who is it?" Suddenly things were looking up; maybe I had my real first suspect.

"Ronald Walton." It was like Katy Lee was talking in slow motion. "He said that he wasn't going to renew the renter's contract."

Suddenly things weren't looking good for Viola White. I had just discovered a good reason for her to kill Doc Walton.

Chapter Twenty-Three

"I didn't think Viola White killed Doc Walton," I said, looking over at Finn, who was hunkered over a plate of the roast beef special from Ben's. "But I'm not so sure anymore."

"I'm not saying she did." He swiveled his counter stool toward me. "Stranger things have happened."

"I hope you two figure out this crime spree quickly." Ben filled up Finn's cup and mine with Coke. "I'm so sick of hearing about it. I'll be glad to get back to hearing the women gossip about each other."

Ben didn't wait to hear a response. He hurried over to greet a couple of people coming in the door.

"I sent in the photos of the tire tracks to a state expert to get an idea on what type of tire and car the tracks might belong to." Finn looked ahead and took a bite.

"That's good," I replied. "I plan on taking them over to Luke to see what his opinion is."

"Have you gotten any more of the evidence reports back?" he asked.

"Not yet. I had Wyatt log and send in most of it." I took a drink.

"What did you have him send off?" he asked.

"The prints we picked up from the scene, though they could turn out to be from patients or Toots. Different blood samples that might not be Doc Walton's. DNA testing from the teeth marks," I rambled, sopping up the juices from the leftover gravy on my plate with one of Ben's homemade biscuits. "I even bagged and had

Wyatt send the glove Doc Walton was wearing to the crime lab, hoping someone's DNA might be there from the struggle."

He nodded his head in approval.

"You showed our entire hand back there at the insurance office." I couldn't believe he told Katy Lee everything.

"I believe in being up front with people. That's the only way I've found that gets people to talk." He ate the last bite of his roast.

He took his napkin out of his lap and stuck it on top of his plate. On a fly-by, Ben grabbed it, throwing it into the bucket of dirty dishes at the end of the counter.

"Everyone is going to know about it at Euchre tonight because everyone talks." I followed his lead and put my napkin on my empty plate.

"We shall see." He smiled. "That's not always a bad thing. It gets people talking and sometimes you might hear something very important to the investigation, when they have no idea how important it is so when we ask them direct questions they leave the details out." He jabbed the counter with his finger. "I have a feeling the smallest of details is going to help us solve the crimes."

He sounded eerily like my Poppa.

"I'll let you know." I took a ten-dollar bill out of my pocket and stuck it on the counter before I got up. "It's time for me to face them. Or you could go for me." I grinned, letting my guard down a little bit. "They would love to see you rather than me. You have charmed them all with your city slicker ways."

"Nah." His eyes squinted when he smiled back at me. "I just follow your saying."

"Saying?" I asked.

"I've heard you say you can catch more flies with honey than vinegar. We shall see." He reached around and pulled his wallet out, pulling out a ten-dollar bill and sticking it next to mine on the counter.

I couldn't help but notice a picture in the plastic part where the license was supposed to go of a very pretty brunette with sparkling teeth like his and her arm snug around Finn's waist, both of them standing on what looked to be a beach, crystal blue water behind them.

My heart suddenly dropped, and I sucked in a quick breath.

"Are you okay, Kenni-bug?" Poppa came to my side.

"So this sweetness to all the ladies is all an act?" I asked, figuring out Finn's game.

"You gotta do what you gotta do to solve the crime, right, Sheriff?" He stood up, winked, and walked out.

"Thanks, Ben," I shouted, a little more loudly than I should've, but Finn set me on fire.

I nearly knocked over the town troubadour and his stupid guitar when I rushed out of Ben's.

I'd been starting to fall for his bullcrap act, just like all the other women in town. With each step to the Wagoneer the madder I got at myself for letting my guard down a little bit.

"I'm so stupid!" I screamed and slammed the door at the same time, hoping the slam drowned out my anger.

"You were listening to your heart." Poppa sat next to me. "You have a little something for that boy."

"No. I don't." My knuckles turned white as my hands gripped the wheel.

"Don't tell me that."

Poppa held onto the door when I turned left off of Main Street, taking a quick right on the town branch.

"I don't have a thing for Finn." I rolled my eyes. "He is going to march right on out of here after we solve the murder, so I can't let myself fall for that perfect smile."

"I wouldn't say that." Poppa's ghost looked a little scared when I brought the car to an abrupt stop right in front of Tibbie Bell's house, flinging us both forward. "You need to cool off. Maybe a little something with this guy is what you need."

I jerked the keys out of the ignition.

"Are you kidding me?" I looked over at him. Through the passenger window I could see Lulu and Ruby standing on Tibbie's covered front porch waiting for someone to open the door, their hands loaded down with food. "First off, no way, and secondly, I don't need advice from my Poppa's ghost on my love life."

I didn't bother waiting for a response from him. I jumped out of the Wagoneer and grabbed my extra clothes I kept in a duffle bag. I made it to the front steps just in time for Tibbie to open the door and let everyone in.

Chapter Twenty-Four

Everyone else had already arrived at Tibbie's for the Euchre game and was mingling around the food. Since I had already eaten supper, I figured I'd just go straight to the desserts after I changed into civilian clothes. It felt good to pull my hair out of its ponytail and let it hang down. I took the pin off my uniform and pinned it on my sweatshirt. I didn't want to lose it.

Maybe being here at our Euchre circle, I could put the crimes and the ghost of my Poppa in the back of my mind. Sometimes when I didn't think so hard, things would just naturally come to me. I hoped this was one of those times.

Just a couple hours with my friends was probably all I needed to feel normal again. What I wouldn't give to go back to forty-eight hours ago when everything was boring.

"Kenni, I'm so glad to see you," Lulu said when I walked into the room where the dessert table was located. She was peeling the Saran Wrap off of the glass plate of chess bars. "I've got an extra plate of chess bars in my car for that handsome cop that's helping you. Don't forget to remind me to give them to you." She pulled her shoulder up to her ears and winked before she rushed off to talk to a few of the other ladies.

I forwent the chess bars, only because Finn had made a remark about them and I didn't want to think of him, and went straight for the peanut butter brownies. One bite and I knew who had made them. Mama.

"I'm glad to see you are eating." Mama's voice escalated. "From the looks of you in that towel, I was afraid you weren't."

I shoved the rest of the brownie in my mouth and turned around, but not without glancing around the room to see if Dr. Houston was there yet. I still wanted to talk to her about our little conversation earlier in the day and see if she'd changed her mind on giving me some names of her clients that had partials and a chipped tooth.

"I'm eating," I said, my voice muffled with chipmunk cheeks. A few pieces of brownie flew out of my mouth. Not to my surprise, Mama scowled, muttering something about manners, and threw her hand out in front of me, a pink and lime green bag dangling from her grip. I tossed my head back. "What's that?" I asked, reluctant to take it.

Anything from my mama always came with a price. I had learned that lesson a long time ago.

"Towels." The bag swayed back and forth like a pendulum, waiting for me to grab it so it could chop off my hand. "I knew you wouldn't run out and get your own, so I went to Lulu's Boutique and bought you a few."

"But not without words!" Lulu yelled from one of the card tables set up in the room across the hall.

"Words?" My brows knitted.

"It's nothing." Mama giggled.

I grabbed the bag and opened it. There were four towels separately rolled and tied with a pink and lime green bow. I pulled one out and sat the bag next to my feet before uncurling it.

I had to admit, I liked the heavy cotton and the length was far longer than I was used to. I jerked the corner up to get a look at the monogram, only it wasn't monogram.

"'No holes?'" I asked, reading the words.

"It doesn't have any."

Mama reached around me and grabbed one of Lulu's chess bars.

"Clever, Mama." My lip quivered as I tried not to smile. From what I could recall, this was the first time in a long time Mama had tried to make a joke.

"See." She reached out and placed her warm hand on my arm. "I can be witty."

"Funny, not witty." I patted her hand, a peace offering for the night.

"And if you just so happen to have an overnight guest," her voice escalated, "he will have a towel to use."

"Mama." I tilted my head. I knew she was talking about Finn without her even having to say his name. "Are you kidding?"

"Well, he is a cutie." Mama shrugged and quickly walked away. She always had to have the last word. "Plus, I can tell by how you look at him that you are a wee bit interested." She held her finger and thumb an inch apart and up to her eyes before she turned and walked back into the game room.

I grabbed another brownie and stuffed it in my mouth.

A couple of other ladies came into the room and put a few items on small plastic plates. I moved to the side to make more room.

"I wouldn't pee in her ear if her brain was on fire," Ruby quipped, before snatching off a pig in a blanket hors d'oeuvre. "After all, she is her mama up one side and down the other."

"Uh-huh." Stella from the church circle nodded her head and piled one of everything up on her plate. "I about died when I pulled my cart right on up to the belt and placed my milk on it and heard her voice."

"And that hair." Ruby fluffed her bright red hair with the edges of her fingers. "It's maroon and purple mixed together."

"I'm telling you—" Stella started before Ruby interrupted her.

"She's just like that no good mama of hers."

Ruby nodded her head several times before Stella nodded back.

I wasn't sure if Stella was being polite by giving Ruby the head nod back; Ruby's nod was her way of telling Stella this conversation was between them. But we all knew it was Cottonwood gossip and would be spread around like manure.

"Whose voice?" I butted into a conversation I wasn't even

privy to. But I knew Stella and Ruby. They both loved to flap their jaws and a little bit of gossip might do my soul some good.

"Kenni, honey." Ruby's face held surprise. "I didn't see you standing over there. Like you're hiding or something."

I smiled. "I'm not hiding." I reached over and grabbed one of the pigs in a blanket. "Just grabbing some food when I heard you talking about somebody that I can only figure to be Toots Buford."

It didn't take a genius to know who had purplish hair around town. Only one person, and that was Toots.

"You can't take us two old hens seriously." Stella's face quivered. The circles around her eyes deepened even more when she tried to smile.

"Who are you calling an old hen?" Ruby jumped around, flipped Stella off, and stomped off into the card table room.

Stella's neck slowly moved up and down when she swallowed. I was good at reading people, and I was good at making them nervous.

"I'm glad Toots got her job back at Dixon's Foodtown." It was a big relief knowing the death of Doc Walton didn't leave her without a job.

"She sure was rootin' tootin' mad and let everyone know how she got fired." Stella leaned in. "I even found a business card of Dr. Shively in my grocery bag when I got home." She pulled back, her eyes drawing down, and she tugged on the hem of her cardigan. "I know I didn't put that business card in my basket."

"What do you mean fired?"

My mind was still trying to wrap around the first sentence Stella spouted.

"Doc Walton fired her a week ago when she didn't put away the files like she was supposed to." Stella shrugged. "Not that I'm gossiping or anything, but you are the sheriff and Doc Walton is dead."

"Are you sure?" I asked, knowing Toots was the second person at the crime scene, other than Sterling Stinnett.

"Hand to God. Over a week ago." She threw one hand on her

chest and one hand up in the air. "You know I'm a Bible-fearing woman. I would not pack a tale."

"Oh, yes you would." Poppa stood behind the dessert table. "I sure would like a piece of your mama's peanut butter brownies. You know it's a family recipe straight from my grandmother's cookbook."

"You are sure she was fired over a week ago?" I wanted to make very sure because this was the first I'd heard of it.

If that was the case, why was she at Doc Walton's? Had she really come up on him? Was she really the one who killed him and when Stinnett found him, she was hiding? Maybe the tire marks had nothing to do with the murder. I mean, if Toots was mad about the firing, she could've confronted him that morning, stabbing him out of malice. Toots wasn't very strong and the stab wounds weren't deep. And she did have access to those thermometers. Heck, she could've bought thermometers at Foodtown.

Laughter brought me out of my thoughts. Viola White was sitting at one of the Euchre tables with my mom. She was grinning from ear to ear since she and Mama had just taken a trick from their opponents.

I looked back at Stella.

"I'm telling you, she was cussing Doc Walton up one side and down the other about how he fired her because she left out an important client file and he said how if it got into the wrong hands someone's life would be altered forever." Stella's plate teetered, full to the brim, and she kept piling more on.

"Whose file was it?" I asked.

"I have no idea." She shook her head. "Toots said she wouldn't tell me, but it would come out soon enough." Stella shook her finger at me. "Now this is between me and you."

Slowly I nodded. I couldn't wait to tell Finn. What did this mean? My heart raced. My nerves were on edge. Not only did Viola have a good motive to kill Doc, now Toots did too.

"I'm starving," Stella said before she turned and headed back into the card table room, nearly knocking Tibbie over.

"Sorry, Stella," Tibbie apologized after she rounded the corner so quickly without looking. "Okay, come on," Tibbie said to me and pointed to the room with all the players, trying to get me in there so I could start my game.

"Good work, Kenni-bug." Poppa bent over the plate of brownies and took a nice long whiff. "You might have a shot at this sheriff thing after all."

Toots Buford had never been on my mind as a suspect. She'd gone from not being on the radar at all to being at the top of the list alongside Viola.

I stood in the doorway looking into the room at all the women. My eyes zeroed in on Viola. I just couldn't imagine her stabbing someone. She smiled. Her teeth were nice and straight. Did she have a partial?

I took my phone out of my pocket and sent a quick text to Finn.

Just found out that Doc fired Toots over a week ago. Why was she at his house the morning of the murder? Stop by her house and see what she has to say about that.

He replied quickly: *Will do.*

Chapter Twenty-Five

"Kenni!" Jolee smacked the table between us. I jumped in the air along with my nerves. My head wasn't in the game. I tried my hardest to listen in on Mama and Viola's conversation, and my hand was on my phone. I couldn't wait to see what Finn had found out from Toots. "Are you wanting me to pick it up?"

She brought my attention to the King of Hearts sitting on top of the kitty pile.

Though it would have been a strong trump card, there was no way I was going to tell her to pick it up when I had a handful of low cards in all four suits.

"I mean, it's a big one," Jolee coaxed, her lashes wide open.

"I'll pass," I whispered and fell right back into my thoughts and the possibilities of Toots being the killer.

She might have a reason to have killed Doc Walton, but what was the connection to White's Jewelry?

Viola White was Euchre partners with my mama and I could easily mosey over there and drop a few questions.

"Kenni?" Jolee questioned my move of over-trumping her when I didn't need to.

I raked the pile close to me and smacked down a nine of hearts, which was clearly not going to win the hand.

"It's all I got." I shrugged and got up from the table, knowing I had just thrown the game and our chance of moving on with the quarter tournament.

"What is with you?" Jolee settled back into her chair, a little disappointed. "I haven't seen you this scattered in a long time."

"It's this case." I glanced over at Viola White, knowing I was going to have to seize the opportunity to ask her about the insurance. It was lucky she'd stepped up to the plate to be Mama's Euchre partner since Missy Jennings was sick. "I'm racking my brain about who and why someone would want Doc Walton dead."

"Don't you let this community stop you from investigating and doing what you need to do to bring the killer to justice." A smile crossed Jolee's face. "And maybe you need to do some late night rap sessions with one Finn Vincent."

"It's not like that." I could tell her mind was playing some type of romance scene in her head. "Besides, he's not interested in me. And if he was, I'm not interested in him or a relationship."

My heart fluttered and I put my hand up to my chest.

"Not interested, huh?" Jolee's eyes focused on my hand.

"Heartburn," I lied. "I always get heartburn after eating too many of my mom's peanut butter brownies. Can you let Duke out for me after this?"

"I'm surprised he isn't with you." She stood up and pushed her chair in.

"I wasn't sure how many stops I needed to make and keeping him in the car isn't fair to him."

"I'll let him out." Jolee dropped her hands from the back of the chair. "I'm going to go eat. Are you leaving?"

"I'm going to check on Mama and Viola, then I'm out." I stood up, taking a little courage from Jolee's words about not letting the community stop me. I was going to confront Viola White. Maybe not in front of everyone now, but the opportunity would present itself at some point tonight.

The Euchre games were well underway and everyone was talking about Jolee's and my ten-week winning streak and how it had just come to an end, leaving my mama and Viola in the running for first place. Missy was going to be so mad when she found out Viola was a better partner for Mama.

"I might be old, but I'm going to go it alone." Viola pumped her jeweled hand in the air.

"That's my girl!" my mama screamed with pride. "You got this. I'm going to the bathroom."

Mama got up and I took her seat across from Viola.

Katy Lee Hart and Gina Kim were their opponents and each let out a long sigh along with an eye roll. When someone "went alone" in a Euchre game, it meant they were confident enough to be able to take all the tricks of that hand, winning full points for their team. Mama and Viola only needed to win this last trick to win the game and make it into first place.

When it came to Viola, she was no stranger to going alone and probably a reason they had been in second behind me and Jolee. She was a good stand-in partner when we needed one. She and Mama were vicious tonight and normally that would fire me up to beat them. But not tonight. More important things were on my mind. A killer.

The four rounds of cards were over in seconds.

"Yes!" Viola pounded the table with her hand and belted out the famous line of Queen, "We are the champions, my friend."

"Shut up." Ruby snorted over the top of her spade-shaped glass filled with brandy. "Not for long."

"Long enough," Viola snarled, gathering the deck of cards into a nice neat pile.

Katy Lee and Gina got up, leaving us alone.

"Viola, can I ask you a couple of questions?" I asked.

"Sure, honey." Her hands were busy shuffling the deck and doing all sorts of fancy folding tricks with the cards. "Did you find my big diamond? I told Wyatt it was stolen and I want it back."

"No, I'm sorry, I haven't. Yet. Though it's my understanding that you don't own the building where your store is located, that Doc Walton did." Since she was taking her sweet old time shuffling the cards, I took the opportunity to text Finn.

Did you find anything out?

He answered, *She wasn't home. I left a note on her door.*

I wrote back, *Did Wyatt say anything about that big diamond Viola had in her shop? She said it was stolen during the robbery.*

Not a word to me, Finn replied.

"He wasn't going to renew your contract." I put the phone back in my lap.

"He's a fool," she said. She tapped the edges of the deck of cards, her hands as steady as her voice. "I made him money."

"Don't let up, Kenni-bug," Poppa encouraged me.

I gulped and took a deep breath.

"He said he was going to move his office back into town, when you and I both know he couldn't do that." Her chest bumped out when she let out a puff of air. Her eyes slid from the deck of cards up to my face. "You can't possibly think I murdered him."

She looked at me like I had two heads, appalled I could even think such a thing.

"Well..." I eased back in my chair and glanced around to make sure no one was listening. Everyone had gone to get dessert and spread more gossip. "Anger is a good motive for killing someone, and there was no forced entry into your shop." I bit the corner of my lip and thought for one second about what I was about to say. "Plus, you had a pretty good insurance plan on your jewelry."

"How do you know that?" Her brows knitted in curiosity. "There are only two people who know about my insurance dealings." Her mouth dropped open, and I took the opportunity to take a quick look inside to see if I saw any dentures or partials.

"I am the sheriff. I have to check out everyone who had dealings with Doc Walton, and it sure does seem like you had dealings." I shrugged.

"I don't like what you are trying to say, Kendrick Lowry." Her voice was calm, her gaze steady.

Chapter Twenty-Six

"I don't know what got into me," I groaned, looking down at the tip of my shoe. I shoved my toe in the broken concrete at the threshold of The Tattered Cover Books and Inn, which was next door to Ben's. "It was like I went crazy. I continued to batter her with questions that I should've brought her in for questioning to do. Not in front of everyone."

I looked up and blinked the tears from my eyes, because I wasn't sure if I was seeing things. Finn Vincent stood at the door of his hotel room without a shirt on and his jeans unbuttoned.

The sign in the background illuminated Finn's face, giving it the glow of an angel. Or maybe it was just me hoping he could be my angel and save me from the embarrassment Viola White was about to bestow upon me.

Finn shut the door, leaving me standing there in the night air.

"I'm sorry. I should've called first," I grumbled, turning around to walk down the sidewalk to my car parked down the street.

"Wait." Finn opened the door and stepped out, shutting it behind him. He skipped up beside me. Fully dressed. "I had to put on a shirt." A corner of his lips tugged up, sending my heart into a flutter.

"Shirts are optional in Cottonwood." I smiled.

"Have you been drinking?" he asked, tucking his hands deep into his jean pockets.

"No, but that might help." I shook my head and pointed toward Ben's. He nodded.

"Nah. It will only cloud your judgement even more." He held the door of Ben's and ushered me in.

I stopped in front of him and watched his eyes address my outfit.

"What? This is a Euchre tournament outfit. Comfort." I referred to my jeans and oversized sweatshirt.

"Okay." He shrugged.

He danced around me and pulled a chair out for me at the same table near the window we had sat in before.

"Thank you," I said and blushed.

"I do have good manners," he said and took the seat across from me.

Ben looked over and smiled. Ignoring him, I threw two fingers up in the air.

"Make it three," Finn said getting Ben's attention.

I put three fingers in the air. Ben acknowledged us.

"Okay. What did you do? And is it going to compromise the case?" he asked.

Ben walked over, two cups in one hand for me and one cup in the other for Finn.

"I'll be back with cream." He held a finger up and on his way back flipped the front door sign to "Closed."

"He's closed." Finn started to get up.

"Don't mind that." I waved him to sit back down between sips. "He's used to seeing me here at all hours of the night. Plus, he lives upstairs. I'll lock up on my way out."

Ben ran the creamer over and went back to sweeping the floor, not paying a bit of attention to us. Not much anyway. I did see a couple of glances, but it was probably his curiosity getting to him.

"I pretty much accused Viola White of Doc Walton's murder." The words coming out of my mouth made me sick all over again. "It was horrifying."

"Why did you do that?" Finn looked how I felt. Appalled.

"I was going off the tip that Doc Walton wasn't renewing her lease and her high insurance policy against theft." I paused and took a sip of coffee. "I tried to look in her mouth to see if her teeth matched the bite marks, but I can't tell the difference between real teeth and fake ones."

"After I went to Toots's house and she wasn't there, I went by Cowboy's Catfish to see Wyatt so I could ask him about the diamond. He wasn't there." Finn tapped his finger on the edge of his mug. I noticed he wasn't drinking much. "Have you seen him?"

"No. I know he's probably tired from all the paperwork he had to fill out for the forensic lab. He isn't used to working so much, but we do need to make sure that he filed the missing diamond report," I said. "Viola will hire the best lawyer if we don't file her stolen jewels exactly by the book." Finn was staring out the window. His eyes held a faraway look. I pointed to his cup of coffee. "Aren't you going to drink it?"

"Yeah." He shook his head like he was shaking off an idea. "I was just thinking about something."

"What?"

"Nothing." He smiled from behind the steam coming up from his mug as he took another sip. Then he must've changed his mind. "I looked around Wyatt's desk to see what reports he had filed. I didn't see the diamond file, but I wasn't wanting to snoop either."

"I'll ask him in the morning. I'm sure he did it." I shook my head and let out a sigh. "Viola's got a lot of clout in this town."

Finn nodded. His eyes slid to the pin on my shirt. I raised my hand to touch it.

"I heard you've never really gotten over his death." He gave that empathetic smile that I hated. I was used to that smile from everyone telling me how sorry they were about Poppa.

"My mom?" I asked. I wouldn't put it past my mama to tell Finn everything. She was already scheming ways to get us down the aisle.

"Wyatt," he responded, giving me a little shock.

"Wyatt?" I repeated with a little bit of disbelief.

I took another drink of my coffee and pondered Wyatt's motive to tell Finn about my relationship with my Poppa.

"It's nice to see another side to you." Finn's finger tapped the edge of his cup.

My brows cocked and my head tilted. Anger poured out of my mouth. "I'm not sure why he'd be discussing my history with you."

"Actually, he was saying how this case has made him see glimpses of your Poppa and how great a sheriff he was," Finn said. "I'd take that as a compliment if I were you. And I agree, you are a good sheriff."

Reaching over, he cupped his hand over mine. The warmth of his palm sent an unfamiliar sense of chill bumps over my wrist, up my arms, and down my body.

"I..." I was a nervous wreck. I swallowed. Hard. "I am starting to understand what my Poppa went through."

"No!" Poppa smacked the table, making the coffee cups rattle. My second cup of coffee spilt over the rim. "Do not touch her!"

Finn and I jerked apart.

"What was that?" His brows furrowed.

"Ouch!" My face scrunched up in pretend pain and I stuck my leg out from underneath the table, swinging it back and forth. I rubbed my thigh. "Cramp. Cramp."

I did my best Oscar-worthy performance trying to cover up Poppa's crazy outburst.

"It's the coffee." He pointed between my two cups. "You drink way too much caffeine."

"It's not enough coffee." I swung my body back around and grabbed my coffee, taking a big long sip of it.

Poppa stood next to Finn, taking a good long look at him.

"That was fast." Finn grabbed a couple of napkins and threw the pile on top of my coffee spill.

"What was?" I sopped up the coffee mess and left the saturated napkins in a pile.

"You got over that cramp real fast." He smiled. "Or did my hand make you flinch?"

"Don't be a jerk."

Damn, he was good. Or I was just a bad actor.

"What am I going to do about Viola?" I changed the subject, taking the heat off of my fake cramp.

"Nothing." He shrugged and pushed his coffee away from him. "It's business. You used your instinct and now we can investigate her motive even more."

I eased back in my chair. Finn was right. I had to remind myself that even though Cottonwood was a small town and everyone knew everyone's personal business, they didn't need to know the sheriff's business.

"Maybe he isn't so bad." Poppa bent down and looked directly into Finn's eyes. "I want him to be your partner in your job. Not your life, even though I can see he makes you happy."

Finn blinked a couple of times. His head moved back slightly and he squinted as though he was trying to focus on something in front of him. Poppa.

"Are you okay?" I fished, clenched my teeth, and popped my eyes open and took a long look at my Poppa, hoping he'd get the hint.

"Yeah." Finn rubbed his eyes with his thumb and finger. He squinted a couple of times as though he was trying to get his eyes to focus. His chair squeaked across the old tile flooring when he pushed back from the table. "I'm just tired. I was half asleep when you knocked on the door."

"Drink your coffee." I sighed in relief when he didn't mention Poppa.

Finn was quiet for the rest of the night, even on the walk back. It wasn't an uncomfortable silence because my mind was still going over everything about the investigations.

"Kenni." Finn stopped in front of the Tattered Cover with his room key out and ready. He reached out and put the same warm hand on my arm, giving it a gentle squeeze. "I'm here for you. I have a lot of resources and I know you're holding back on me."

It was the first time Finn called me by my nickname, and it made my heart flip flop.

"I'm not," I pish-poshed his idea. "It's no secret that a small town like Cottonwood likes to gossip, and you just never know who's on your side and who you can trust."

"I'm not from Cottonwood, and I'm not just someone." His eyes were compelling and magnetic. I tried to look away, but my eyes wouldn't cooperate with my brain. "Let me in as a friend. I've found things really click with partners when I'm friends with them."

"I gotta go." I took a step back before I turned around, giving a slight wave. "I'll see you in the morning," I called over my shoulder, not giving him the opportunity to ask me where and what time.

He was finding his way around Cottonwood better than most lifelong residents. Maybe that was what was so appealing to me.

Chapter Twenty-Seven

The light in my kitchen pierced the window and flooded out into my dark side yard. I slowed down when I approached the house, but let the Wagoneer roll on by as I rubber-necked into the windows of my house.

A shadow that was not Duke's crept across the large bay window from my living room. My heart pounded, my palms beading with sweat.

"Poppa, where are you?" I cried out. "What good are you if you can't ghost yourself into my house and see who is in there?"

Was he there to help or haunt me? Right now I needed the help.

"Poppa?" I called out again.

Of course he wasn't anywhere around when I needed him. I flipped the headlights off and rolled down a couple of houses past mine until I came to a complete stop.

I reached under my seat and grabbed my shoulder holster.

"Here I come." I unsnapped my gun from the holster and got out of the car, keeping the gun snug in my two-hand hold.

In the dark of the night, I prowled around in the shadows like a cat, keeping out of the full moon's spotlight. When I got to the side of my house, I made sure to stay low underneath the windows, and headed around the back of the house where I knew my motion light had burned out. It had been on my list of to-dos and now I regretted not working down that list.

The back door was flimsy because Duke always used his paws as a battering ram on it to let me know he wanted to go out. He didn't scratch like most dogs; he ran full force and jumped up, making the screws loosen a little more each time. Tightening the screws was also on my to-do list. Regardless, I rarely locked my doors. Maybe I'd have to rethink that.

Using my dominant hand, I pointed the barrel of the gun down. My thumb was on one side of the grip and I kept my middle, ring, and pinky fingers curled securely around the other side just below the trigger guard. I planted my back up against the brick of the back side of my house, right next to the back door. Slowly I brought the gun straight out in front of me and cupped my other hand around my gun hand to keep me from shaking. It was the first time I had ever come face to face with an intruder, and I wasn't sure how this was going to go down.

When I saw the shadow pass by the light of the kitchen, I made a swift movement sideways, kicking in the door with my right foot, smacking the door open.

"Hold it right there!" I screamed, staring down the sight of my Magnum at the back of someone. The intruder stopped dead in her tracks, arms up. "Mrs. Brown?"

"Goodness, child." Mrs. Brown, my neighbor, turned around and put her hands on her large chest. Her hair was tucked up under a nightcap and her face had paste all over it. "You can't go running around pointing that thing at everyone."

"Mrs. Brown." Confused as to why she was here, I lowered the gun. Duke jumped on me, putting a paw on each shoulder. "Why are you here?"

"Jolee was delivering my Meals on Wheels nightly snack and I told her I was going out for a walk." She shook her bony index finger at me. "She told me not to since there was a killer on the loose, but I said I'm fine because I live right next to Sheriff Lowry and she won't let nothing happen to our neighborhood. And that's when she said she forgot to let Duke out and asked me if I could since I was going on a walk."

My hands were still shaking. Duke wasn't moving. I turned the safety on and set the gun down on the counter.

"I'm sorry. Jolee didn't tell me you were going to let him out." Thank God I didn't open fire on my neighbor. "Thank you. I was just freaked when I didn't see any cars in the driveway and a shadowy figure walking around in here."

"Don't worry about it." Her feet shuffled over to the back door. "I'll be going now."

"I'll walk you home. It's the least Duke and I can do." I looked over at my door hanging off the hinges. That item on my to-do list just became a priority. "Be careful of the door I just broke," I warned and helped her out.

What should have been a five-minute walk took us about twenty. Duke didn't mind. He sniffed, lifted his leg, and peed on everything in our path.

"That dog never runs out, does he?" Mrs. Brown chuckled. Duke had peed on every single bush along her small red brick ranch house. I held the screen door open for her. Her hand shook as she tried to get the key in the hole.

"Polly told me about the robbery." Mrs. Brown turned the key and opened the door. I had forgotten she was Polly Parker's great-aunt. "Would you like to come in?"

"I would like to make sure you are safe and sound." I followed in behind her and Duke darted in too. The smell of mothballs made my stomach curl. "It's the least I can do for you."

"Ask about Polly." Poppa appeared out of nowhere. It took everything I had not to give him a piece of my mind. If he'd shown up when I needed him to, I wouldn't be worried about Mrs. Brown and cardiac arrest.

The morning gossip would be buzzing with the fact that I'd pulled a gun on her, and if going in to make sure she was safe would give her a reason not to rat me out on my behavior, then it was worth it.

"Do you know who broke into Viola's place?" Mrs. Brown shuffled from light to light, flipping them on.

Her house was full of antiques. She could open up her own shop and give Ruby a run for her money.

"I have some good leads, but nothing solid yet." I put the emphasis on yet so not to look like a complete idiot.

"Polly said it shook her up real good." Mrs. Brown and I made our way into her kitchen.

There were papers and books all over her kitchen table, but the rest of the house was spotless.

"What were you looking up?" I asked out of curiosity and took a couple of steps toward the table.

"Polly has been experiencing some strange sensations in her legs and arms, so Doc Walton did some testing and diagnosed her with a genetic disease." Mrs. Brown stirred uneasily around her kitchen. She didn't look at me. "Only we don't have the disease in our family."

"Is it serious?" I asked.

"Enough to put her in a wheelchair at a young age." She picked up a piece of paper with long words written on top of it. "HSP. It stands for Hereditary Spastic Paraplegia."

"Take the paper," Poppa encouraged me.

"I'm trying to figure it out. Her mama is none too happy with how Polly is spending her time with Mayor Ryland." Mrs. Brown huffed and shuffled back out of the kitchen, letting me know it was my time to go.

"She is?" I asked.

"Kendrick Lowry." A shadow of annoyance crossed her face. "I know you have flipped over Polly's life backward and forward to see if she had anything to do with the break-in at White's Jewelry. I know you've figured out there is some sort of relationship between her and the mayor. I told her mama it was because Polly never had a good relationship with her daddy." Mrs. Brown let out a long sigh. "Especially since they had her so late in life."

All the information Mrs. Brown was telling me was being fully recorded in my head.

"No offense, but your niece has pampered Polly into a princess and that includes her daddy. So having her later in life didn't affect their relationship."

"It has more than they let you know." A sneer hovered around Mrs. Brown's lips.

"Can I have this piece of paper?" I asked Mrs. Brown. She simply pushed it toward me. I picked up the paper and folded it, putting it in my pocket.

"Come on, Duke." I patted my leg and he came running. "Good night, Mrs. Brown. Thank you for letting Duke out and I'm sorry about the gun thing. Habit."

"Night night, dear." She shut the door behind me and I was happy to hear her run the slide lock.

The only thing I wasn't happy about was her not saying she wasn't going to tell anyone how I had pulled the gun on her, though I had good reason.

♪

Chapter Twenty-Eight

Early the next morning I took Duke for a run while my morning coffee brewed. When I came back, I surveyed the door to determine how I was going to put a Band-Aid on it until I could take the time to really fix it.

"You did a number on poor old Mrs. Brown." Poppa smacked his leg as he went into a full-on fit of laughter. "I thought she was going to drop a load when you had that gun pointed at her."

"I don't think you're funny." I continued to survey the door and sip my coffee. "You aren't the least bit amusing and you're not helping me." I turned around and put my hands on my hips when I came face to face with him.

I grabbed the paper Mrs. Brown had given me and placed it on the kitchen counter. Somehow I was going to have to add this new information about Polly to the investigation. Not that Polly having a family disease pointed to Doc's murder or the break-in, but I had a nagging feeling that it needed to be looked into.

I opened the cupboard under the sink, grabbing the screwdriver set I had picked up at a garage sale when I moved into the house. I plucked the Phillips head out and did the best repair of the hinges I could until I had real time to devote to it. "I needed you last night. You could've ghosted your way in here and told me that it was only Mrs. Brown."

The more I talked, the harder I pushed the screwdriver in the stripped screw and turned faster.

"Wait." It had just occurred to me: I didn't need any dang warrant; I had Poppa. "I need you to do something."

"Do what?" He had a hurt look on his face.

"You zip in and out of places and no one but Duke and I can see you." The idea of having Poppa be a fly on the wall started to sound really enticing. "I want you to go to Camille Shively's office and search through her files. See if anything pops out at you."

"I guess I could." Suddenly color came back into his face and the sneaky smile I loved grew across his lips. "And this will ramp up the investigation."

"I won't be able to prove what you find without the warrant and file in my hand, but you will definitely help speed up the investigation." People would really question how I got my hands on information without the warrant and an investigation on me would be the last thing I needed.

"I'm not a bad carpenter." I swung the door back and forth. It was a little lopsided, but it was on the hinges and in working order until I could find the time to replace it.

"Where do you go when you aren't with me?" I asked, easing down in a chair at my kitchen table and drinking more coffee. "If you're going to be my ghost partner, then I think you need to tell me."

"If you must know," Poppa whispered as though he were hiding something, "I was at Luke Jones's house."

"Why were you at Luke's?" I asked, knowing he was on my list of people to see. I had to get his opinion on those tire tracks.

"*Gunsmoke*." Poppa dropped his head. "I'm a sucker for Audie Murphy."

He was. Every Sunday I would go to Poppa's house; it was his day of rest and he watched western movies all day long. The 1953 classic happened to be one of his favorites.

"Luke is showing *Gunsmoke*?" I asked. Poppa nodded. "Early bird special too?" He nodded again. I looked at the clock on the stove. I loved popcorn for breakfast. I filled Duke's bowl with a bunch of kibble and made sure he had a full bowl of water.

"You stay here." I gave him a good rub on his head and grabbed my gun and keys. "Come on, Poppa. We're going to the movies."

Chapter Twenty-Nine

"Movies?" Poppa asked once we got back in the car. "I thought we had other people to talk to about the murder."

The pink Beetle caught my eye in the Dixon Foodtown parking lot. I whipped the Wagoneer into the parking lot.

"What are you doing here? I thought you said movies," Poppa screamed, holding on to the handle on the side of the passenger door as if I was about to kill him. "Grocery shopping should be the last thing on your list when there is a killer on the loose. You are burning good daylight."

"If I'm going to the movies, I need to get me a Diet Coke. There is something just not right about eating popcorn without a Diet Coke."

I kept my eye on Toots's VW Bug.

"Popcorn for breakfast?" Poppa questioned.

"And there's no time like the present to question Toots Buford about Doc Walton firing her and the fact that she left out that bit of information." I jerked the Wagoneer into the space next to Toots's car. Maybe she could let me in on why she was at Doc's office that morning.

"It's a little tight over here." Poppa looked out the window at the space between my car and Toots's.

"Well, good thing you're a ghost and you can just whip on through."

The sign on the door informed customers of their safety, that

Dixon's was taking extra precautions by having extra lighting in their parking lot and Baskin's Security had installed better surveillance cameras.

"Hmm..." I tapped the sign. "Little do they realize, Toots just might be the one they are ramping up their security for."

"You never know. It is strange she was at Ronald's when she was fired." It was good to hear Poppa working again. I had always loved how he would talk out his ideas with me when he had a case.

My parents begged him to stop telling me about the bad criminals of the world and said he was going to corrupt me, but I loved it and had to believe I might have helped him figure out a few things. Now was no different.

"Her reasoning could hold a lot of the answers you need to solve Ronald's death," Poppa said, pointing to the cashier's station.

"I have to buy something besides a Diet Coke," I said to Poppa, trying to figure out what I could buy that wouldn't make Toots run off and tell the town council that I was harassing her at work.

"Duke needs a bone."

"Perfect." I snapped my fingers and walked down the produce aisle.

A familiar voice came from the next aisle over. It escalated with each word.

"One of these days I'm going to get out of this crazy town!" The shrill voice was none other than Polly Parker.

"You'll thank me one day," her father growled.

"No, I won't."

Polly sounded even angrier.

I put my ear up to the piled papayas, parting a few so I could hear them a little clearer.

"Your mama and I have done the best we could by you and you have been nothing but ungrateful. You think you can go around doing whatever you want to whoever you want," Mr. Parker said in a hushed whisper.

Silence stood between them, but after the sound of a squeaky cart passed, they started up again.

"When your mama and I heard about what happened, we knew it was you," he said.

My ears were perked up more than Duke's when I gave him a juicy ham bone. I leaned a little closer until I was practically laying in the fruit.

"Is it telling you it's ripe?" a guy with a Dixon's Foodtown apron asked, causing me to jump around, sending the piled up papaya into an avalanche.

"Oh no." I put my hand out, willing them to stop to no avail. They continued to tumble and tumble until there wasn't a papaya left in the bin.

Poppa was cracking up as the papaya gathered around his feet. He kicked one toward me. The produce worker watched as the solitary papaya rolled toward me after the others had rolled away from me.

"That must be the one." I reached down, grabbed it, and tossed it in the air before catching it with one hand. "My dog loves papaya."

I didn't look back. I decided against the bone. It was best I got in Toots's line and out before Polly and her father saw me.

Toots looked none too happy as she ran the items across the scanner and the cash register beeped. I grabbed a Diet Coke from one of the mini coolers on the end of Toots's line.

"Will this be all?" Toots asked before she looked up.

"Fancy seeing you here." I slipped a few dollars out of my pocket and smacked it on the conveyor belt. "I had no idea you were working here again."

"I haven't been back long." Toots's face was pasty white against her maroon hair.

"I'm glad I ran into you. Saves me a trip to your house." I looked behind me to make sure there were no customers, especially the Parkers.

"Why?"

Her lips smacked together.

Another customer came up behind me and started unloading

their grocery cart on the conveyor belt. "Where will you be around lunch time?"

"I'll meet you at Cowboy's Catfish." She didn't bother telling me to have a good day or even goodbye. She simply took the first item of the customer behind me and ran it across the scanner.

Chapter Thirty

"I wonder what Polly Parker and her father were talking about," I said to Poppa on our drive over to Luke Jones's house. "He said that once they heard, they knew it was her. Do you think they were talking about the jewelry store? Do you think Polly did it? She has this disease. How does that affect her?" I sucked in a fast deep breath and let my thoughts roll out of my mouth. "And what does it have to do with Doc Walton if we are trying to tie her to the murder? According to Mrs. Brown, Doc knew about the disease." I snapped my fingers. "Poppa, do you think Polly went to see Camille Shively because of the disease? Maybe Polly told Doc Walton she was going to get a second opinion."

"Doc was very protective of his patients and his diagnoses." I loved how Poppa and I played our ideas off of each other. "I wouldn't put it past Ronald to have confronted Camille Shively like it's been reported."

"That's whose file you have to find." I felt like a piece of the puzzle had just clicked into place. "You have to go to Camille's and look for her file."

"I do think there is something very fishy between Polly and Toots." Poppa squirmed around in his seat as if he was uneasy. "I think you're on the right track about the files. I just have a sneaking suspicion that one might be taking up for the other. They are best friends. But who is the killer?"

"I think you're on track. Something is odd." My head turned side to side trying to find a parking spot. I couldn't drop the idea that maybe Polly's secret was in those files. The conversation between her and Camille Shively wasn't far from my memory.

The street in front of Luke's was lined with cars. I recognized most of them. One of them was Wyatt's. *Gunsmoke* was a popular movie in Cottonwood. Most westerns were. I took a couple trips around the street to see if anyone had left yet and left a vacant parking spot, but no such luck. I had to park around the corner and walk.

"You know, I was looking around," Poppa said. "And I saw some posters for the *Summer of Sam* movie."

"You did?" I didn't recall Luke ever showing that movie.

"I did. It looked like he showed it around a year ago. It might be something to ask him about since you are here. Maybe see who was there?" Poppa made some good suggestions.

"I'm not real sure what it has to do with the crimes, but there might be a correlation since the Chinese symbol was found at both crime scenes. How does this tie into Viola, Toots, and Polly?" I tucked Poppa's information in the back of my head.

"I found clues in places I never thought would pan out. This could be a good lead." Poppa was right. Sometimes the strangest ideas brought clues I'd never thought of. "You just have to eliminate one person at a time."

We made our way to the back of Luke's house to the basement door. The big sign above the door was lit up. It said "Shh," which meant the movie was in progress.

I slipped in, sticking a couple of dollars in the donation box, and grabbed a popcorn from Vita, Luke's wife.

"Sheriff." Vita greeted me with a smile.

"Is Wyatt here?" I asked, squinting through the darkness.

"He's up in that group somewhere." She pointed. "They come for all the westerns. But they never give good donations. I told Luke to charge them, but he doesn't." She groaned. "It might not cost a lot to run a reel, but it costs something."

"I'm sure it does," I agreed with her. "Thank you, Vita."

I held the bag of popcorn up to my lips and grabbed a piece

with my tongue, flipping it in the clutches of my teeth. Mmm...there was nothing better than a perfect piece of buttery, salty popcorn.

I picked a seat right behind Wyatt, who was sitting behind the mayor. He and the other men didn't notice. There were a few people scattered here and there, but I couldn't tell in the dark who was there and who wasn't.

Mayor Ryland didn't even try to whisper. "Viola White called me saying Kenni accused her of killing Ronald while they were playing Euchre."

"She did what?" Wyatt jerked to the side to face Mayor Ryland.

"Yeah." Mayor Ryland let out a puff of air in a laugh. "I wish I could've voted you in as her deputy. That way you could keep an eye on this investigation."

It took everything I had not to come to my own defense.

"She's doing a fine job. She's using Finn, and he's doing a good job too," Wyatt took up for me.

"Shh." A voice from behind me pierced the darkness.

"It doesn't stop there." This time Mayor Ryland whispered, forcing me to lean in a little more. "Viola also said that Patty Brown called her and said Kenni pulled her gun on her." Mayor Ryland shook his head. My jaw dropped. Did she leave the part out that she was in my home?

"I'll talk to her." Wyatt took a handful of popcorn and shoved it in his mouth. I wished he'd shoved it in the mayor's face.

Fifteen minutes into the movie, I looked to the back of the room where Luke and Vita were busy cleaning out the popcorn machine. It was probably the only opportunity I was going to have to ask him about the tires and the *Summer of Sam* movie.

Mayor Ryland glanced over his shoulder when I got up and the chair squeaked. Luckily, he didn't turn completely around and see me.

"Kenni, I didn't know you were here." Luke poured butter into the popcorn machine. My mouth watered. "I keep a close eye on who comes to see what their tastes are so I can get movies everyone likes." There was pride on his face.

Luke and Vita were good people.

"It looks like a great crowd for the early showing." I kept my voice down so I wouldn't bring attention to us. That was the last thing I wanted to do.

"These old westerns always bring in crowds. I didn't take you for a western kind of girl." He opened the Morton's salt container and practically poured the entire thing into the popcorn machine.

"I'm known to watch a western or two since my Poppa loved them." I smiled, recalling the fond memory. "But I'm really here to ask you a couple of questions about some tires."

"The Wagoneer really can't go wrong with the Dunlop. A little pricey, but well worth the wear and tear you put on your car with your job." He nodded his head. "I bet you could get the town council to vote and use the town funds to purchase them."

"I'll keep that in mind, but I'm here to ask about some tire prints I found at Doc Walton's."

His face clouded with uneasiness. He motioned for me to follow him out the door and I did.

"I'm asking for your opinion since I believe you're the expert in all things cars, not to mention movies." Stroking his ego was my way of buttering him up like he did the popcorn.

Luke's chest puffed out; he tried to contain his smile as he tugged on the waistband of his jeans. His upper lip curled as he took a deep breath of pride.

"I do know a lot about cars."

"Yes, you do." I snapped my fingers and pointed at him. "That is why I came directly to you."

I pulled my phone out, found the pictures Finn had emailed me, and let him take a good look at them.

"May I?" he asked, gesturing to hold my phone.

I handed it to him. He flipped through the pictures and I waited for his response.

He let out a lot of groans and grunts along with a few huhs. A few times he tapped a picture and acted as though he was going to say something, but then kept it to himself.

"Very interesting. I believe these are tire tracks from a fifteen-inch Le Castellet wheel. Very rare; I've never seen a set around Cottonwood." He continued to look at the photos. "I've only seen photos since people around here don't drive foreign cars."

"Foreign?" I asked.

"You know, we all drive Fords or Chevys." He laughed. "But this type of tire is from a B3 G60 Syncro Passat." He showed me the photo. "Volkswagen, small station wagon type of car."

"You've never seen this type of car or tire around here?" I asked again to make sure I heard him right. I had to wonder if this was someone who was traveling through and committed both crimes.

"Never." He pushed the forward button and looked at the next photo. "Oh my God." He gasped, his eyes looking up at me hollowly.

"What?" I asked, taking my phone back. The picture of the Chinese family symbol on Doc Walton's wrist was on there. "I didn't mean for you to see that." I stuck the phone back in my pocket.

"What the hell was that?"

"You are still under the law, so this stays between me and you. Now that I have your expert opinion on these tires, I'm more convinced than ever this was not someone in our community and may be someone who is on a crime spree across the state."

Boy, was I getting good at making stuff up. But I had to do what I needed to do to get him to believe how important it was to keep quiet. I decided to take the opportunity to ask about the movie *Summer of Sam*.

"Say," my eyes lowered, "have you ever shown the movie *Summer of Sam*?"

He nodded. "Yeah, about a year ago."

"You did?" I asked. "I don't remember that, and I usually have your schedule posted on my refrigerator."

"It was only one night because it got stolen. It was the only film I had on DVD." He rolled his eyes. "Go figure."

"Can you recall if Polly Parker came to see it?" I asked,

wanting to have a connection between her and the crimes as well as Poppa's claim that she stole a movie.

His lips pursed as though he was remembering something. Slowly he nodded his head. "She was here, come to think of it. Not many people were, but she stuck out because I didn't figure her for a gory girl."

"Huh." I scratched my head. My internal alarm went off.

Polly Parker was becoming more and more connected to the crimes. First the break-in; then she was adamant the crimes were tied to the new condo complex by Doc Walton's, as though she was trying to get the heat off her; plus her disease Mrs. Brown told me about. But why would she kill Doc? Surely a second opinion on her disease wasn't a good enough motive for her to kill. Something was missing.

It was proven most of Doc's stab wounds were shallow, and Polly wasn't strong. I had said the same for Viola and Toots. But I needed hard evidence. Everything I was going on was circumstantial, not enough to arrest someone.

A knife sticking out of his neck. Chills overcame my body and I found myself shaking in my shoes when I remembered Betty Murphy's words when she called me over the walkie-talkie. Where was that knife? There was no knife when I went to the scene. The only person in there was Toots.

I gulped. Was Toots an accomplice? I recalled going to Camille's and hearing Polly Parker's voice in the exam room next to me. Maybe Polly was upset about the disease this whole time.

"Say, doesn't Polly's father have a bunch of cars?" I'd always heard Mr. Parker had a garage just for his vintage cars.

"Yeah, but he doesn't let me work on them. He sends all of them to those fancy dealerships." He scoffed. "Spends money like it's water."

"Thank you for your time." I had to get out of there. I had to figure out how to put Polly Parker at the crime scene. I was more convinced than ever that she was the killer. Luke put his hand in the air before he walked back into his basement.

Polly Parker was mad. Doc Walton diagnosed her with the disease. The family disease, which was where I could connect the Chinese family symbol. Her father owned fancy cars, which would explain any strange and unusual tire marks. She killed Doc Walton in a fit of rage, and though I still couldn't explain the mercury, I would. Then she called Toots to help her. Toots came to take out the knife and panicked when Sterling Stinnett showed up. We wouldn't think it was strange she was there because we thought she still worked for Doc Walton. While Toots was there covering for her best friend, Polly let herself into White's Jewelry where she staged a break-in so she'd have an alibi to place her at White's. But where was the diamond?

Polly Parker killed Doc Walton and Toots Buford was an accessory to murder. I was more convinced than ever.

"Sheriff?" someone called out into the night air as I made my way back to the car. "Can I talk to you?"

Sterling Stinnett stepped out from behind one of the tall oak trees that lined the sidewalk in front of Luke's.

"Sterling." I was relieved to see it was just him. "Sure."

"I wasn't sure how to ask this, but I was at the town meeting when Finn was voted in as your deputy." He scuffed the toe of his beat-up shoe on the ground, his head down. "I was wondering if I was still helping out like y'all asked. I mean, if you need me." He lifted his head. His eyes dipped down. "I sure did like helping out. I felt important."

"Yes." I nodded, not wanting to hurt his feelings. "I definitely need all eyes and ears on the lookout for anything. You understand?" I asked.

"Yes, ma'am." He smiled. "I'll keep my eyes and ears to the ground like a good hound dog."

"Thank you so much, Sterling." I waved over my shoulder on the way back to my car.

Chapter Thirty-One

I didn't get too far down the road when my phone rang.

"Hello?" I answered.

"A good lead just came in." Wyatt didn't bother greeting me with a hello. I could hear the movie in the background. He just dug right on in. "I got a call from Shirley Babbs."

"Who's that?" I asked and pulled the Jeep to the side of the road. I grabbed my pen and notebook out of my bag and wrote down everything he was telling me.

"She owns the pawn shop in Clay's Ferry and she heard about the jewelry store robbery at White's. She said she had some new pieces that looked too nice to be secondhand." He talked and my mind raced.

Pawn shops kept really good records.

"What's the name and address?" I asked, then wrote down the information he gave me. "Have you gotten any of the results from the evidence back yet?"

"No, but I'll check on that today while you check out the pawn shop." He was really helping me out. It was refreshing to finally have someone on my side. "Wait," he corrected himself, "there was nothing on the surveillance tapes from Doc Walton's. He hadn't even bothered recording."

"He must've scared off the coyote." That was the only reason I could figure Doc would stop recording, just like Art Baskin had said. "If this pawn shop lead pans out, then we won't have to worry about the video. Keep your fingers crossed," I said, crossing my own fingers like Wyatt could see through the phone. I didn't bother telling him my hunches about Polly. If this Shirley could identify Polly, we would have a strong reason to arrest her.

"I feel like you're really close, Kenni." Wyatt's words comforted me. "Your Poppa sure would be proud of you."

"I am." Poppa appeared in the passenger seat, smiling. "In fact, Luke did identify the make of the tires, so that should help out a lot."

Wyatt and I said our goodbyes.

Quickly I dialed Finn. He didn't answer so I left him a message telling him to meet Toots at Cowboy's Catfish and ask her about her job at Foodtown and why she had left that out in her statement.

"Let's go." Poppa sat in the passenger seat and tapped on the dash. He pointed his finger forward. "Go!"

"Feels almost normal." I smiled over at him. It felt like old times. "You're really here, aren't you?"

"I am." His eyes slid up to mine and held them. "I don't know why, but after you got elected sheriff, I was able to watch over you like a guardian angel. I have no idea how long I'm here, but I'm enjoying working with you."

"I'm glad you're here." A sudden peace came over me, as if a warm blanket was cocooned around me. "I'm really glad."

"Let's go." I put the Jeep back in gear and headed out of Cottonwood toward Clay's Ferry. I could tell Poppa wanted me to solve the crimes as much as I wanted me to.

"You know," Poppa shook a finger at me, "something is just off with all of this." He shook faster. "I just can't put a finger on it. But we will, Kenni-bug. We will."

The pawn shop parking lot was empty. I parked right next to the door. Shirley Babbs's shop was just as gaudy as most of the jewelry in her cases. There was nothing there that screamed White's Jewelry to me.

"What can I do you for?" Shirley stood behind the counter, her jaw flopping open and shut with each crack of her gum. Her hair was piled high on her head, her long nose a little off-center on her thin face.

"I'm Sheriff Lowry from Cottonwood. Wyatt Granger told me that you called in about some jewelry." I planted my palms on the glass counter and leaned over, looking at the locked-up case.

"This in particular." Like slow motion, she put her hand in her pocket, pulling out a strand of pearls with a monogram circle charm on the end. "When she brought it in, she was crying, saying she needed the money." She laid it on the counter. "Most of the time I don't get in monogrammed items, but this is a real set of pearls. When I got the police report about keeping an eye out for jewelry that might be pawned, this little baby was on there." She tapped her finger on the circle charm. "A dead ringer for the one listed on your report."

"I didn't put it on the report." I bit my lip, realizing my mess-up. The initials read PP. I had forgotten to add to the report that Polly was missing her infamous pearl bracelet. The bracelet she claimed was stolen. Thank God either Finn or Wyatt had heard me ask her and put it in the report. If they hadn't, we would've never gotten this tip. "What else did she bring in?"

"This is it." She shrugged.

"Nothing else?"

Shirley slowly shook her head, then suddenly stopped. She straightened up. "I asked Dale and he didn't get anything else either."

"Dale?" I asked.

"Yep, my boyfriend comes in to look after the place when I go down to the tanning bed for a half-hour break." She patted the side of her cheeks with her hands. "I feel better with a little color on me."

"Back to Dale," I said, trying to get her back on track.

"Oh, Dale." She grinned and let out a happy sigh. "He said we got in a piece of jewelry that might be on the list, but Mr. Granger didn't recognize the description on the report."

"Do you have the piece?" I asked.

"I don't. Dale sold it on consignment before I got back. Then a couple of days later, I got your report." Shirley picked up a cleaning cloth and a bracelet. She rubbed the gold bracelet back and forth, making it as shiny as the bright summer sun.

"Is this the girl that came into the shop and pawned the stuff?" I asked and pulled out the file I'd been compiling on Polly Parker. Granted, it was an old picture, but she didn't look any different.

"Yes." Shirley looked at the photo, and then pushed the bracelet toward me. "That little girl sure didn't look like a killer or jewelry thief to me."

"Killer?" I asked.

"It's no secret that the two are probably tied together. I read it online in the *Cottonwood Chronicle*."

Of course Edna Easterly had already printed something in the *Chronicle*.

"Thank you for contacting us." I slipped a card out of my bag and handed it to her. "If you or Dale think of anything else, please call me."

"I will."

Shirley chomped while looking at my card.

With the bracelet in hand, I knew it was time to confront Polly. I was going to her house. If her father was there, it'd be a bonus because I could question them about their hushed conversation in the canned vegetable aisle at Dixon's Foodtown.

Twenty minutes later, Poppa and I pulled up in front of the Parkers' gated mansion. It wasn't far off the road and I was sure the Parkers did that to show off. They had a circular drive with a wrought-iron gate on each entrance. There was a large lake in the middle of the drive. Four concrete swans as big as my Wagoneer spit water out of their beaks from the middle of the lake. The mansion was the most modern building in Cottonwood and the Parkers didn't keep it a secret that they paid just as much for the design of the house as it cost to actually build it.

"And just how are we going to get in there?" I bit the inside edge of my lip and scoured the surrounding area with my eyes. The Parkers wouldn't be like Doc Walton and cut their cameras. "Well, like Finn said, sometimes you just got to be frank with people."

"After all, you are just checking on their precious Polly since she was involved in a terrible robbery," Poppa added.

"You're right." Sarcasm flowed out of my mouth. "She was so distraught over being violated."

I rolled down the window and pushed the little black button on the call box.

A red light on top of the box began to flash at a rapid pace.

"Show off those pretty teeth Beverly Houston gave you. Your parents paid an arm and a leg for braces." Poppa gestured to the camera.

"Can I help you?" someone asked through the box.

"Sheriff Lowry to see Polly Parker," I stated.

"Hold on please." The box screeched like my walkie-talkie. The small red light went off.

Poppa and I waited patiently for a couple of minutes and I pushed the button again.

The person finally came back. "I'm sorry, Miss Parker is not in."

"That's fine. I'll see Mr. Parker. So you can open the gate or the front end of my Wagoneer will do it for you. Either way is fine with me." I hated to get a little demanding, but I'd had enough of the Parkers thinking they were above the law.

A loud buzzing sound came from the speaker and the gates began to slowly move outward. I put the Wagoneer in gear and waited until the gates had stopped opening before I proceeded up the drive.

"Seriously," I looked out the windshield at the massive house, "what is it like to have this much money?"

"A burden." Poppa was right. The Parkers had a certain standard they liked to portray and it had to be exhausting trying to keep up. "You're doing just fine in my old house."

"You're right." I put the Wagoneer in park. "I wouldn't ever move out of that house, even if I won the lottery."

Calm came over me as I looked at Poppa. Normally when I had to go on a call or interview someone, I would be a nervous wreck.

But with Poppa here next to me, though no one else could see him, I felt so much more at ease. Maybe it was his advice, but even just having him there gave me a little more confidence. And that was exactly what I needed to solve these crimes.

"Sheriff." Mrs. Parker's pruned-up face always looked like she was smelling something bad. Her nose was always curled, her eyes squinted, and her mouth pursed. Her brown hair was cut into a chin-length bob and not a single strand was ever out of place. She, like Polly, always wore pearls. I'd bet they even slept in them.

"Mrs. Parker." It was best to keep it short and sweet. "I wanted to make sure Polly is doing okay."

"I'm going to look around while you keep her busy." Poppa disappeared into the mansion, leaving me on the front porch with Mrs. Parker.

"Won't you come in?" Mrs. Parker took a step back. The heels of her shoes clicked on the marble flooring.

There was a maid standing behind her.

"Please go get the tea set," she told the maid. "I'm assuming you do drink tea."

"No." My answer would be the talk of the gossip circle. Everyone in Cottonwood drank tea.

She drew back like I was being rude. She was really going to think I was rude when I handed Polly an orange jumpsuit to wear in prison.

"Never mind, Miranda." She turned and I followed her into the front room, where there was only a couch and two chairs. Minimally decorated. "Please sit."

I sat. My knees were shaking. I really hoped Poppa could find something that would help out.

"Where is Polly?" I asked.

"She and her father took one of his cars to the dealership. It's a rare car he doesn't drive anymore, so he will probably trade it in for something wonderful for Polly." She eased down into the chair next to mine, crossed her ankles, and folded her hands into her lap. Her head turned and she glanced out the window. "Polly has been having a tough time with the break-in. In fact, it's made her a little more defiant."

"I'm sorry to hear that." I wasn't. I was happy to hear they were at a car dealership because I could trace any sort of transaction they would have with the dealer, not to mention get records from the county clerk's office on the type of vehicle and its taxes.

The tires and the bracelet would definitely link Polly to the murder and the theft.

"Do you know if Polly remembers anything else about the robbery?" I asked, trying to buy time for Poppa. I glanced over to the door to see if Poppa would appear.

"No." Mrs. Parker looked back at me. Her eyes held a sadness. I wondered if she knew Polly was having an affair with Mayor Ryland.

I pulled the pearl bracelet out of my pocket, dangling it in the air between my fingers.

Mrs. Parker gasped. She reached out to get it. I pulled it back.

"Evidence." I didn't tell her that Shirley had ID'd Polly to a tee. "I wonder if someone is trying to frame Polly as the thief. Does she have any enemies? I mean, I just couldn't imagine, she's always been so nice to me."

As nice as a piranha. I glared at Mrs. Parker.

"I think it's time for you to go." Mrs. Parker stood up and walked out of the room toward the front door.

"Yeah. Let's go." Poppa didn't bother waiting for me. He disappeared as fast as he'd appeared.

"Thank you for your time." I turned away from the door to face her. "Please tell Polly I'm looking for her. Official business."

"Are you telling me that my daughter is your number one suspect?" Mrs. Parker asked.

"Yes. That's exactly what I'm telling you." I took a step backward, out of the door.

"And to think we voted for you," Mrs. Parker huffed and slammed the door in my face, nearly smashing my nose.

"That didn't go so well." I slammed the door after I got back into the car.

"I think it went great." Poppa smiled, pleased as a peach. "While you were in there, I went to check out those files in Camille's office like you had asked me to after I didn't find anything in the Parker's mansion."

"And?"

"Ronald had run a full panel on Polly's DNA, which was in both his and Camille's files. Camille had only run a panel for that specific family gene. Ronald had another piece of paper in there that read 'Paternity Test.' The name was blacked out, but there was a number." Poppa rattled off the number.

"Paternity test?" I questioned. "Mrs. Brown said something about family secrets. I wonder..." I tapped the wheel. "Did the papers have the testing lab on it?"

"DNA Diagnostics. The same one we use for the sheriff's office." Poppa grinned.

"It looks like I'm going to have to make a little visit." I put the Wagoneer in drive.

"That's not all." Poppa's face was gray. "It's also in Polly's records that when she was a kid, she had an accident at the pool where she slipped on the concrete, knocking some of her permanent teeth out."

"She has a partial?" My mouth dropped. I'd never've guessed. Poppa nodded his head. Things were becoming very clear.

On my way back to Clay's Ferry, I called Finn again.

"Finn, I haven't heard from you today. I wanted to make sure you met with Toots. Also, I just got some more information that you will find very interesting." I debated on whether to leave the information on the message. "Give me a call. I'd rather tell you and not your voicemail who I think the killer is."

Chapter Thirty-Two

The lab was in a brown brick building. I hadn't been there since I became sheriff, but I'd gone with Poppa many times when he was sheriff.

"How can I help you?" A gray-haired man walked out into the waiting room after the doorbell above the door dinged when we walked in.

"I'm Sheriff Lowry from Cottonwood and I am here to look into some DNA paternal lab results that were run here by Doctor Ronald Walton." I pulled my photo badge from my pocket. Sometimes it wasn't enough to have on a uniform.

"I can't believe this old son of a gun is still here." Poppa took a good look at the elderly man in front of me. "Tom Geary."

"Mr. Geary." I put my hand out. "I bet you don't remember me." I sure didn't remember him, but Poppa did and it was time I threw some granddaughter genes around. "I'm Kenni Lowry, Elmer Sims's granddaughter. I use to come around here with him when he was sheriff of Cottonwood."

Tom Geary looked me over. His brows narrowed.

"I'm so glad to see you are still here and processing all of our testing."

He softened. "Do you have the number on the DNA testing?"

Poppa rattled off the number again and I rattled it off to Tom.

"You have a good memory." He turned and had me follow him to the back.

We walked over to a desk with a computer. The wall behind him was glass and behind that was the lab. There were a couple people who were covered head to toe in surgical scrubs, masks, and gloves working in the lab.

"Tell me that number again." He typed as I said the number yet again.

"Here we go." Tom took a closer look. "I'm guessing you don't have a warrant."

"You guessed right, but I can get one." I sighed.

"Well, I might as well give you what you need. I know you'll be back with a warrant so we can skip that part." He hit another button on the keyboard and the printer turned on.

He walked over and grabbed the paper the printer had spit out.

"Here are the DNA results Ronald Walton ran." He showed me the paper. "Here it shows the patient tested positive for Hereditary Spastic Paraplegia, HSP for short. It looks like there was a DNA test run on the mother and father." He pointed to Polly's parents' name. "When they didn't turn up as having the genes the patient needed in order to have HSP, Ronald ran another test."

Tom paused.

"He had me run his own DNA." Tom handed me the paper.

I didn't need him to tell me what the paper said.

"Are you telling me that Ronald Walton is Polly Parker's real father?" The words coming out of my mouth shocked me.

"What?" Poppa's eyes darted back and forth from me to Tom.

"Yes." Tom Geary had just sealed the case.

"Here is my cell number." I scribbled it on a piece of paper on his desk. "Please call me as soon as the other evidence Wyatt had you process is finished. I need it ASAP."

Tom just looked at me as I hurried out of the lab.

Chapter Thirty-Three

"Doc Walton is Polly's father." I couldn't stop saying it. "Her father."

The information was having a hard time sinking into my thick skull.

"And that gives her a reason to kill him and tells us why the shop was broken into. She stole her own jewelry and a few items from the store so it looked like it was a break-in." I smacked my hands together. "The family symbol. I knew that was the key to this. Polly found out when that Mr. Parker wasn't her real dad by the DNA testing." My mind continued to put together a plausible reason for Polly to have killed Doc. "Polly confronted her mother about the disease. Her mom knew that neither Mr. Parker nor herself had the disease. It was then that Polly realized Mr. Parker wasn't her father and her mother had to come clean." I continued to put the clues together. "That explains the stab wounds not being so deep. And since Doc wasn't the strongest of men, elderly, Polly was strong enough to break the thermometer and hold the mercury beads up to his mouth after she had somehow wrestled him to the ground." I tapped my finger on the wheel. "And we can't forget about the teeth."

"That's where she went wrong. A good criminal would never do anything to give herself away. She wanted revenge for not only her mother's affair, but for giving her the HSP." Poppa still looked shocked.

"And that explains the post-mortem stab wounds. Polly was angry with him." I started the car and grabbed my phone.

When the jail's answering machine picked up, I left a message. "Wyatt, since you aren't at the jail, I'm going to run by your house. I hope you're there. I know who killed Doc Walton, the motive, and why they broke into the jewelry store."

"I knew you could do it, Kenni-bug." Poppa and Duke both sat in the passenger seat.

"I couldn't have done it without you." I pushed the pedal down to the ground. I couldn't wait to get to Wyatt's. He was going to be just as happy as I was that this was a solved case.

Thank goodness I was the law because I drove as fast as I could, disregarding the speed limit. I had to get to Wyatt's so we could get our warrants in a row and put Polly Parker behind bars without any backlash from her father. Mr. Parker had a way of making things disappear and I was sure if I didn't cross my T's and dot my I's on this case, he would find some sort of loophole and she'd never be brought to justice.

No wonder Mrs. Parker didn't want to talk to me. No wonder Polly had gotten defiant. There was no doubt in my mind that the Parkers would do anything to keep this little family secret buried in the backyard. Even murder.

I made it back to Cottonwood in record speed.

"Lookie there." Poppa pointed at the small station wagon when we pulled up in front of Wyatt's house. "B3 G60 Syncro Passat, and the tires are muddy."

"And the mud came from the back of Doc Walton's house." I knew I had her. "Polly and Mr. Parker must be in there with Wyatt. I can't let them leave. We need to enter the tires as evidence."

I pulled past Wyatt's house and parked on the street a couple of houses down. I grabbed my bag and took out the camera. If anything happened to the car, I would have pictures. I made sure my gun had bullets and slipped my shoulder holster around my chest, snapping it snug.

"It's time to give Polly her bracelet back and give her the bad news," I said to Poppa. He was raring to go and already out of the car waiting on the sidewalk.

In an ideal confrontation with a criminal, I would prefer to have backup. My only hope was that Wyatt was there.

When we got up to the car, I snapped several pictures of the tires from all different angles. I glanced around the street and didn't see Wyatt's car.

"Where's Wyatt?" I asked Poppa.

"How would I know?" He shrugged. There was an irritated look on his face. I watched as he looked around. "Something isn't right."

"You feel it too?" I asked, and sat the butt of my hand on my gun. "Something's going on in there."

Poppa put his finger to his lips. He tiptoed to the back as if someone was going to hear him and I followed, only I had my gun out and gripped.

I busted in the back door with my gun stretched out in front of me.

"Where is Wyatt?"

Polly Parker was sitting at Wyatt's kitchen table; Wyatt's gun-cleaning kit was strewn out along with his shotgun.

"What is wrong with you, Kenni? I swear." She grabbed the barrel of the gun. "You've lost your mind."

"Put the gun down now!" I jabbed my gun toward her. "I know all about your disease and Doc Walton being your daddy and the lengths you've gone to make sure no one knows."

Her face turned fifty shades of red, ending in pink.

With one hand on my gun, I slipped the pearl bracelet out of my pants pocket. I swung it in the air.

"This little baby was your mistake. You thought you could take it to a pawn shop to get rid of the evidence." I buried it in my palm and grabbed the butt of the gun to steady my shaking hand. "Wyatt!"

Polly put her hands in the air and slowly stood up. "Wyatt isn't here. He and my dad went to the store. Why don't you sit down and let me explain?"

"No." I waved my gun for her to sit back down. No wonder

Wyatt's car wasn't there. "You sit down and I'll tell you how things are going to go down."

"You can't tell my dad." Polly's eyes teared up and her face started to contort, reminding me of her mother's. "He doesn't know he isn't my father."

"Did you call Toots and tell her about how you killed Doc Walton because you found out that he was really your father and he had HSP, the same disease you have?" I asked through gritted teeth, never once taking my eyes off of her. "I know Toots was fired and she'd do anything for you. Did she go back to the scene of the crime and try to cover up your mess? Did she take the knife out of his neck? The knife you used to stab into his already dead body? How did you use the mercury? I never figured you for that smart."

I painted a bleak and ugly picture with my words so she could visualize the evil she had done in her pretty little head.

"My parents took a break!" she screamed, pounding her small fist on the table. "They were on the verge of divorce and she went to see Doc Walton for medication to help her with depression. That horny old man took advantage of her!"

Polly's shoulders slumped and she fell to the floor, sobbing uncontrollably. She might have gotten some sympathy if Wyatt was home, but she wasn't getting any from me.

"So you went to see Doc Walton about the results and found out he was your father. Then you went to work and made it look like a break-in. Sick! You pulled a Son of Sam and drew the Chinese family symbol on him and the floor of the jewelry store. Then you pawned your bracelet so it looked like a thief did it." I kept my gun on her.

"I pawned my bracelet to pay for the genetic testing so I wouldn't use my parents' insurance. I didn't want them to find out so I paid for it myself," Polly said in a shaky voice, her eyes staring at the gun.

"Oh, how convenient. A little too tidy, if you ask me." I'd heard enough. It was time to get this crime in the books. "Polly Parker, you are under arrest for the murder of Doctor Ronald Walton."

"What is going on here?" Wyatt stood at the back door, his mouth open, his eyes wide. "Kenni, put the gun down."

"Wyatt, keep her father out of here." I kept my gun on her and didn't move. "She killed Doc Walton because he was her father. She found out and went nuts. When she realized what she did, she wanted to make sure she wasn't a suspect, so she ransacked White's and took the jewelry to the pawn shop." I used one hand to pull out the bracelet and tossed it to Wyatt. "You were right. Shirley ID'd Polly just like we thought."

"Wyatt?" Polly lay limp on the ground. Her head tilted up. "You think I killed my own father? Where is my dad?"

"I'll cuff her," said Wyatt. Taking one hand off my gun, I jerked my cuffs off the strap on my shoulder holster and tossed them to Wyatt.

"Are you sure about this?" Wyatt asked and bent down next to Polly. "I left her dad at the dealership. He's buying a new car."

"Cuff her," I growled, glaring at the cold-blooded killer.

"Polly didn't kill anyone." Poppa stood in the hallway next to Wyatt's kitchen. I turned my attention toward him. "You need to go to the bathroom."

Wyatt took the cuffs and did what I told him.

"What?" Nothing was adding up. Everything pointed to Polly Parker.

"Kenni-bug, calm down. Take a breath. Gather your wits. Polly didn't do it," Poppa insisted. "Go to the bathroom."

I looked between Wyatt and Polly a couple of times before I dropped my gun to my side and walked back to Wyatt's bathroom.

"What are you doing, Kenni?" Wyatt asked, walking on my heels. "Kenni, you need to go see a doctor. I think you're losing it."

Poppa stood over the bathroom countertop. He pointed to the medicine cabinet.

"Kenni." Wyatt's voice hardened. "Don't."

My eyes drew down to the sink where there was denture cream and a box for dentures. I grabbed the cabinet door and opened it. Quickly I scanned down all of the empty prescription bottles with

Doc Walton's name on the label. Rows and rows of empty Oxycodone bottles. I grabbed the last bottle and held it up to the light. Little balls of mercury filled it halfway. My eyes glanced down at the trashcan where shards of glass glistened.

"What is this?" I asked, unable to believe what I was seeing. "Did you break a bunch of thermometers and collect the balls in this bottle?"

"Kenni." Wyatt stuck his hand out in front of him. "It's not what it looks like."

"It's exactly what it looks like." Poppa pounded his fist in his open hand and ghosted himself out of the bathroom.

"What is this?" I repeated, picking up the trashcan.

"Kenni!" Poppa yelled from the other room. I ran out into Wyatt's office. There was a picture of Wyatt Granger with the B3 G60 Syncro Passat, smiling proudly standing next to it. In an open white jewelry box sitting by the photo was Viola's big diamond. "Wyatt is the killer."

"Oh, Kenni." Wyatt had followed me to his office. A grin crossed Wyatt's face.

"It's okay, Wyatt. We can get through this." I sucked in a deep breath, hoping he'd buy my sensitive side and I could gain control of the situation.

"I don't think so." Wyatt wagged his finger in front of me. "See, I can't just let you go now, Kenni. It's a shame that our sheriff is going to be found dead in a murder-suicide. Since you uncovered Polly and Doc's secret, it gives Polly a motive to kill him and now you and herself, because she just couldn't bear the humiliation this is going to bring to her prestigious, squeaky-clean image. Though she is screwing our mayor." Wyatt let out a bitter laugh.

"Wyatt." I had to buy some time. The evidence I had collected and Wyatt's reaction to all of it swirled in my head, making me sick to my stomach. "We can get you out of this."

"Oh, yeah. Jailer kills doctor, because the doctor gave him all the drugs in the world until he got a conscience and decided not to prescribe any more to him. That will not make a good headline,

Sheriff." Wyatt lifted his pant leg and grabbed his handgun out of his ankle strap. There was also a knife strapped around his calf.

"Oh my God." My hand flew up to cover my mouth. The harder I tried to hide my feelings, the more I couldn't. "Is that the knife?"

"It is." Wyatt shook his head, pride on his face. "Did you think I was stupid enough to leave it at the crime scene?"

"You saw *Summer of Sam* at Luke's. You've been planning this for a long time and had Polly Parker in your mind as your fall guy. Her father is one of your best friends." Bits and pieces of evidence were coming together in my head, finishing the puzzle.

"Your father is also one of my best friends." His evil was showing. "Don't worry. I'll comfort your daddy and your mama."

"You know you'll never get away with this," I warned. "Finn Vincent knows about the evidence. Your tire tracks left at the crime scene. Everything."

"I wouldn't worry about him." He walked over and shoved the gun in my ribs. I grimaced in pain. "I assured him that you and I had this under control this morning. I saw him at Cowboy's waiting on Toots while you went off on the wild goose chase to the pawn shop. It was lucky that I had decided to drop by the office. If not, Finn Vincent would still be in Cottonwood. I called the reserves and thanked them for loaning him to us while we were between deputies and that the case was solved."

He pushed the barrel of the gun deeper into my ribcage.

"Move it. I've got to get this done before Pete Parker gets back with his new car. Polly didn't want to go and it was the perfect opportunity for me to kill her, but then you showed up."

Polly Parker was eerily quiet when we walked back into the kitchen. Her eyes were fixed on the gun Wyatt had stuck in my back.

"Small-town secrets have a way of bubbling up to the surface," Poppa said and smiled before he walked off into thin air.

"Don't leave me now!" I screamed, just as Wyatt flung me to the ground next to Polly.

Chapter Thirty-Four

Polly held up better than I thought she would as Wyatt took pleasure and time in tying the two of us together. I grabbed her hand and gave it a good squeeze. It was my way of telling her it was going to be okay. I was going to get us out of here somehow.

I cussed my Poppa up and down in my mind. He might have helped solve my case, but he sure wasn't helping save my ass.

"You are too damn nosy," Wyatt spat as he stomped back and forth in front of us. "Why couldn't you just leave well enough alone? I planted all the evidence to point to her." He jabbed his gun toward Polly.

Her body flinched. I could feel her fear.

"Now I have to kill you, and that makes three people." Wyatt slid his finger across his throat. On instinct, I gulped. Then he smacked his own head with the butt of his handgun, screaming in pain as the blood trickled from the gash. He talked as the blood worked its way down his face. "I had to save myself because Polly smacked me with my own gun." He unloaded the bullets and bent down, shoving the handgun in Polly's cuffed hands, forcing her to get her prints on it.

He stood back up and grabbed the shotgun she really had been cleaning for him off the kitchen table and slowly loaded it bullet by bullet. He cocked it.

"Shotguns make nasty wounds." He grinned. "But it's all in self-defense, since I know Kenni went to see your mama. The little whore called your fake daddy while we were at the dealership." Slowly he pulled the shotgun up to his face and looked down the barrel. "After this mess is cleaned up, I'm going to resign as jailer. I'll make a great sheriff."

I could make out the gleam in his eye as he zeroed in on me. A pool of blood that had not yet congealed dripped from his head into a small puddle on the floor.

Out of nowhere, Sterling Stinnett swung a baseball bat right at the knees of Wyatt Granger, sending him to the ground in a thud. Wyatt scrambled for the shotgun, but Sterling stomped his foot on it, pinning Wyatt's hand.

"Good work." Finn Vincent stood in the door, out of breath. His eyes focused on mine and relief settled on his face.

My Poppa stood behind him with a smile that reached clear to his heart.

Chapter Thirty-Five

The festival went on as planned. The sun and seventy-degree temperatures allowed the muggy mess at the fairgrounds to dry up and the ground was firm for the fun rides. I had even gone to my parents' house for dinner before I went to the festival to meet up with Tibbie and Katy Lee.

"I guess I haven't thanked you properly." I handed Jolee a couple of dollars to pay for two caramel candied apples, handing Finn one. I wanted to know all the details about how he found out I was at Wyatt's. I had to drag him away from my friends, who were hanging out by the beer tent.

"You don't have to. That's what partners do." Finn took the apple. The touch of his fingers on mine sent an electric jolt through me.

"We are not partners." I tried to be the hardass I was when I first met him, but I was afraid I was losing my edge. "I guess you're going to get back to the Kentucky Reserves since Wyatt is now behind bars. How did you figure out it was Wyatt?"

It was a question I hadn't yet asked him since the arrest of Wyatt Granger for the murder of Doctor Ronald Walton through mercury inhalation poisoning, after Doc cut off Wyatt's prescription drug supply he'd been using to feed his addiction.

"It was the strangest thing." Finn bit into the apple. Juice rolled down his chin and out of instinct, I lifted my napkin to his face and gingerly wiped it off. He grinned. "Thank you."

"Yeah." I played it off. "You were saying?"

"I went to the new condos to follow up on what people around here had said about them, but found nothing. Everyone who lived there was nice, so I decided to head to the jail to see what was going on with the evidence. I found the file Wyatt had compiled for the evidence lab. He sent the evidence off, but checked the box to not process the evidence. It didn't make sense. Then I went to see Toots. She said she went back to Doc Walton's to get Polly's file from him since Polly had gotten the DNA test. She didn't want to see him. Toots and Sterling were just there at the wrong time. Then I went back to the Cowboy's Catfish where Bartleby asked me about the murder. He said he didn't see anything fishy over at the jewelry store, just Wyatt checking the business like he had done every morning; only that morning, he was doing it a little earlier than normal. I found that odd. Then my evidence report came back from the tire tracks. I knew from talking to Wyatt while I've been here that he loved cars and he told me he owned a B3 G60 Syncro Passat."

"That's how you knew he was guilty?" I asked.

"I had a hunch. I was going to see if Doctor Walton had a file on him, but that was when Sterling Stinnett came running up to me in front of Cowboy's Catfish after I had gotten a call from the reserves saying the crimes had been solved." He ran his hand through his hair. "I told Sterling the investigation was over, but he insisted that he'd walked by Wyatt's house and heard screaming. I got in my car and Sterling ran back to Wyatt's, obviously making it there faster than me." He laughed. "I still don't know my way around this little town. I had no idea Wyatt's was right around the corner."

"I'm glad you listened to Sterling," I said. "All of it started to add up when I was at Wyatt's house accusing Polly of all the crimes. I realized it was strange that Wyatt had beat me to the crime scene when he never gets up that early. And he was quick to point fingers. Then there was the evidence I had to stay on him to send to the lab." I shook my head. "He was definitely planting the seeds to make it look like Polly did everything. The White's Jewelry break-in was perfect. Plus, he used the family symbol to tie in Doc's murder."

"Pretty brilliant." Finn nodded. "Wyatt was coming back to the house to kill Polly and blame it on self-defense since all the evidence pointed to her. He was going to let his secret get buried with her."

"I'm glad Viola got all her jewelry back. He must've been frantic running around to all those different pawn shops," I confirmed.

"Good job." Finn grinned.

I grinned. Finn pointed to the Ferris wheel.

"Want to ride?" he asked.

"Why not?" I took a bite of my apple and followed him. "Everyone will come looking for us."

"Let them."

Silently we waited for the next open bucket on the Ferris wheel. The operator told us when to hop and quickly slammed the rod across us, locking us in.

Cottonwood looked so pretty from way up in the night sky. I could see my friends were still gathered at the beer booth.

"Well, thank you." I felt a warm glow inside me. "Now that you're going back to the reserve unit, I'm sure your girlfriend will be happy to see you."

"Girlfriend?" He looked at me.

"I couldn't help but see the picture of the pretty brunette in your wallet when you paid the other day at Ben's." It was tattooed on my brain.

"Kenni." His arm wrapped around my shoulder. "That is my sister."

My face flushed. I felt so stupid.

"You act like you care."

There was amusement in his eyes.

"I don't," I spat, lying through my teeth.

"You're lying." He laughed. "Kenni, would you like to..." He stopped talking when the Ferris wheel stopped, interrupting what I thought might be an invitation to a date. My heart hammered out of my chest.

Mayor Ryland and Polly Parker stood next in line to get on.

"There you are." Mayor Ryland approached Finn and me before Finn could finish his question. I wanted to give the mayor a big shove. "I've been looking all over for you."

"Here I am." Finn put his hand out and they did the guy handshake thing. Polly and I politely nodded at each other. There was an unspoken bond between us now.

"We are having an emergency town council meeting tomorrow night." The mayor spoke with a loud, commanding tone.

"We are?" I asked. Why was I always the last one to know?

"We are. I'm proposing Finn Vincent stay in town and be voted in as the permanent Deputy Sheriff."

"Really?" Finn asked. "Cottonwood has grown on me." He put his arm around me and squeezed. Just then, my parents walked up.

"Mama. Daddy." I blushed. Daddy looked at Finn's arm around me, giving him a look.

"You must be Finn." My daddy stuck his hand out.

"Yes, sir. I am." Finn and Daddy had a good handshake.

"It's nice to finally meet you." Daddy was giving Finn the onceover. He could always tell when I was falling for a guy.

Finn slowly took his arm from around me when Mama grabbed him, inviting him to Sunday dinner after church.

"I'm proud of you." Daddy smiled. "I told your mama I was tired of hearing complaints about the career path you took." Daddy pulled me in for a hug. "You are a damn good sheriff. It's in your blood."

"Thanks, Daddy." I still had to look up at him. He made me feel like a little girl.

"Kenni." Betty Murphy ran up to us. "Where is your police radio?"

"I left it in my car. Why?" I asked. The look on her face frightened me to my core.

"Come quick! Myrna Savage from Petal Pushers Landscape

called. There's a dead body in her greenhouse!" Betty screamed.

I pushed past her, forgetting all about Finn, and ran as fast as I could to the Wagoneer.

I jumped in, rolled down the window, grabbed my police beacon, licked the suction cup, and smacked it on the roof of the car. The passenger door of the Wagoneer opened.

"You think you're going without me?" Finn jumped in.

My tires squealed on my way out of the fairgrounds parking lot.

"Well, I guess my business here isn't done yet." My Poppa sat in the backseat with a big grin on his face.

TONYA KAPPES

Tonya has written over 20 novels and 4 novellas, all of which have graced numerous bestseller lists including *USA Today*. Best known for stories charged with emotion and humor, and filled with flawed characters, her novels have garnered reader praise and glowing critical reviews. She lives with her husband, three teenage boys, two very spoiled schnauzers and one ex-stray cat in Kentucky.

Henery Press Mystery Books

And finally, before you go...
Here are a few other mysteries
you might enjoy:

LOWCOUNTRY BOIL

Susan M. Boyer

A Liz Talbot Mystery (#1)

Private Investigator Liz Talbot is a modern Southern belle: she blesses hearts and takes names. She carries her Sig 9 in her Kate Spade handbag, and her golden retriever, Rhett, rides shotgun in her hybrid Escape. When her grandmother is murdered, Liz high-tails it back to her South Carolina island home to find the killer.

She's fit to be tied when her police-chief brother shuts her out of the investigation, so she opens her own. Then her long-dead best friend pops in and things really get complicated. When more folks start turning up dead in this small seaside town, Liz must use more than just her wits and charm to keep her family safe, chase down clues from the hereafter, and catch a psychopath before he catches her.

Available at booksellers nationwide and online

Visit www.henerypress.com for details

BOARD STIFF

Kendel Lynn

An Elliott Lisbon Mystery (#1)

As director of the Ballantyne Foundation on Sea Pine Island, SC, Elliott Lisbon scratches her detective itch by performing discreet inquiries for Foundation donors. Usually nothing more serious than retrieving a pilfered Pomeranian. Until Jane Hatting, Ballantyne board chair, is accused of murder. The Ballantyne's reputation tanks, Jane's headed to a jail cell, and Elliott's sexy ex is the new lieutenant in town.

Armed with moxie and her Mini Coop, Elliott uncovers a trail of blackmail schemes, gambling debts, illicit affairs, and investment scams. But the deeper she digs to clear Jane's name, the guiltier Jane looks. The closer she gets to the truth, the more treacherous her investigation becomes. With victims piling up faster than shells at a clambake, Elliott realizes she's next on the killer's list.

Available at booksellers nationwide and online

Visit www.henerypress.com for details

DOUBLE WHAMMY

Gretchen Archer

A Davis Way Crime Caper (#1)

Davis Way thinks she's hit the jackpot when she lands a job as the fifth wheel on an elite security team at the fabulous Bellissimo Resort and Casino in Biloxi, Mississippi. But once there, she runs straight into her ex-ex husband, a rigged slot machine, her evil twin, and a trail of dead bodies. Davis learns the truth and it does not set her free—in fact, it lands her in the pokey.

Buried under a mistaken identity, unable to seek help from her family, her hot streak runs cold until her landlord Bradley Cole steps in. Make that her landlord, lawyer, and love interest. With his help, Davis must win this high stakes game before her luck runs out.

Available at booksellers nationwide and online

Visit www.henerypress.com for details

THE DEEP END

Julie Mulhern

The Country Club Murders (#1)

Swimming into the lifeless body of her husband's mistress tends to ruin a woman's day, but becoming a murder suspect can ruin her whole life.

It's 1974 and Ellison Russell's life revolves around her daughter and her art. She's long since stopped caring about her cheating husband, Henry, and the women with whom he entertains himself. That is, until she becomes a suspect in Madeline Harper's death. The murder forces Ellison to confront her husband's proclivities and his crimes—kinky sex, petty cruelties and blackmail.

As the body count approaches par on the seventh hole, Ellison knows she has to catch a killer. But with an interfering mother, an adoring father, a teenage daughter, and a cadre of well-meaning friends demanding her attention, can Ellison find the killer before he finds her?

Available at booksellers nationwide and online

Visit www.henerypress.com for details

MURDER IN G MAJOR

Alexia Gordon

A Gethsemane Brown Mystery (#1)

With few other options, African-American classical musician Gethsemane Brown accepts a less-than-ideal position turning a group of rowdy schoolboys into an award-winning orchestra. Stranded without luggage or money in the Irish countryside, she figures any job is better than none. The perk? Housesitting a lovely cliffside cottage. The catch? The ghost of the cottage's murdered owner haunts the place. Falsely accused of killing his wife (and himself), he begs Gethsemane to clear his name so he can rest in peace.

Gethsemane's reluctant investigation provokes a dormant killer and she soon finds herself in grave danger. As Gethsemane races to prevent a deadly encore, will she uncover the truth or star in her own farewell performance?

Available at booksellers nationwide and online

Visit www.henerypress.com for details

PUMPKINS IN PARADISE

Kathi Daley

A Tj Jensen Mystery (#1)

Between volunteering for the annual pumpkin festival, and coaching her girls to the state soccer finals, high school teacher Tj Jensen finds her good friend Zachary Collins dead in his favorite chair.

When the handsome new deputy closes the case without so much as a "why" or "how," Tj turns her attention from chili cook-offs and pumpkin carving to complex puzzles, prophetic riddles, and a decades' old secret she seemed destined to unravel.

Available at booksellers nationwide and online

Visit www.henerypress.com for details

FIC KAPPES

Kappes, Tonya,

Fixin' to die

APR 07 2017

CPSIA information can be obtained
at www.ICGtesting.com
Printed in the USA
LVOW10s1038020417
529322LV00008B/422/P